Listening

A Story of a Therapist's Zero Hour

CATHERINE WOODWARD SCOTT

BALBOA.
PRESS

A DIVISION OF HAY HOUSE

Balboa Press books may be ordered through booksellers or by contacting:

Balboa Press
A Division of Hay House
1663 Liberty Drive
Bloomington, IN 47403
www.balboapress.com
1 (877) 407-4847

Print information available on the last page.

ISBN: 978-1-5043-8012-6 (sc)
ISBN: 978-1-5043-8014-0 (hc)
ISBN: 978-1-5043-8013-3 (e)

Library of Congress Control Number: 2017907079

Balboa Press rev. date: 05/23/2017

The author wishes to thank Justin Streeter, Ben Streeter, Leslie Varela, Joanne Greenburg, and the Fireside writers, Fran Jenner, Katherine Hahn, Bob Miller, all my Al-Anon pals, Chris & Dan Gray, Colorado Independent Publisher's Association, Dori Painter, Julie Ramsey, Renn Riley, and Nick Zellinger.

Chapter 1

Boulder Ride

On a clear Saturday morning in June of 2012, a tall bay gelding called Skywalker strode into downtown Boulder, Colorado with Jillian Nicholson easy astride him. They cut a striking figure – he a regal almost-black beast, she a lovely forty-year-old in outsized Jackie Onassis sunglasses, black Stetson on flowing blond hair, and skimpy scarlet bikini.

She breathed in the spring aromas from this higher perspective – fresh-mown hay, lilac, early morning earth, Skywalker's hide and tack – then cozied her bum a notch deeper in the saddle, grateful. At home they rode bareback, she and Sky, their trust secure over these long years of exploring the red rocks of home, the open trails of the Rockies foothills. But this was city walking and that meant saddle.

This was going to be a beautiful day. She smiled and tilted her face into the sun, free hand spread on Sky's wide neck, other hand holding the reins lightly. She caught the stare of a drive-by gawker and gnawed off a bit of cuticle. A horn tapped a brief 'hi-girl' when it got by, likely someone she knew. *Sure hope that wasn't a client. This is a bit much to explain in a clinical setting . . . oh well. All part of this whacko wager.*

But those prickly goosebumps broke out on her flesh despite the warming sun. *Man – I might just as well be naked up here. God. That Doc stood at that mic and dreamed up the perfectly titrated torture for a shy introvert. Who knew the simple human act of turning forty could pack such a wallop?*

Sky walked on imperiously, head held high, tuned only to his love of being anywhere with her and the task at hand of keeping her safe. He snorted and shook his head in his happy coltish way.

"Damn I feel naked, buddy," she told him, free hand massaging his powerful withers.

He nickered in response.

*Good thing I stuck one of Jordan's long shirts in my pack to cover my butt. I **need** a hard core coffee to break up this morning. And those gourmet dinners arriving every day for a month from Doc's wife? Now **that** is gonna ramp this naked caper right up into de**lic**ious.*

~ ~ ~

On her birthday party morning she had tilted her face in close to the bathroom mirror to examine a new wrinkle. Wide green eyes looked straight into her, a small pert nose, rosy full lips with a dimple on the left, a few freckles, not unpleasing face, maybe a little beautiful with that clear skin and highlighted blond wavy thick shoulder-length hair?

She groaned inside. *But gross, this aging thing sucks. Okay talk to me, girl. Stock-taking time on my only ever 4-0 - and rigorous honesty, dammit. So - a private psychotherapy practice of fair repute that I built from nada. Check. Excellent parents, sister still talking to me, and a marriage that works. Check. I gotta say that's a decent body in that mirror. Check. People say I'm the same in or out of the office, pretty real, pretty down to earth.*

So what's eating my lunch? Oh, just that I feel flippin' catatonic at freaking forty. Milestone birthdays bite. Wait - didn't I just go through this - could it have been a decade ago? She cupped her breasts, cranking them up where they used to ride and smiled wickedly. *I don't have to like this. How did Jordan do it? Because he's not a neurotic freak, is how. He just rolled with it all. I hate that.*

Her husband Jordan appeared behind her in his skivvies and held her naked shoulders firmly. *How does he always know,* she wondered. "Look, Jillie-my-love. Right there, Kookaburra. What you see there is the real deal and getting better every single day." He slid a hand to her still flat belly, sending curls of desire shivering through her. "I believe in you now and I always have, damnit, butt-ass nekked, zits and all. We're as good as we are at forty so **deal** with it." He smacked her bare butt as she leaned in to ferret out the zit.

They locked eyes, holding it, matching smiles playing at the edges of their mouths. Familiar, seasoned, satisfying. She grabbed his hand and pulled him toward the bed. "We got time to put out that fire you just lit before this shindig, dawg."

~ ~ ~

Rocking to the clip-clop of Sky's rhythmic walking through the early morning streets, Jillian remembered her birthday party when the dancing got wild and Doc Jackson strolled to the mic to make his killer dare. She never saw it coming.

He signaled the deejay to muffle the tunes, then stood looking around until the silence got everybody's attention. "Listen up all you dancin' fools! So, birthday girl! I'm seeing a vision of you atop Skywalker in that scarlet bikini of yours, ridin' into town for, say, a month of gourmet dinners by June's end? Hunh? What think you, party-mongers? Can you see it?"

How red hot my face got as my friends whistled and fist-bumped. You creeps! And I fed and watered you real nice. I don't believe this – the perfectly hideous nightmare – the precise formula for death by shame. I don't think I can . . .

She took the mic and shook her head at him, eyes closed tight, grinning. "I'll just have the root canal without anesthesia behind door two," she had mumbled into the mic. The crowd cheered her on. "Go Jillie go!" and "Call his bluff, girl!"

Her sister Callie had pulled her aside later. "You don't have to do this, you know, O Introverted One. You sure it's worth a month of divine dinners to you?"

"It's like this, Cal. Doc is daring me to stretch myself, to show up like the Madonna on a winged beast and somehow keep breathing." She blew kisses to imaginary fans. "I'll show the s-o-b." She flicked her fingers from under her chin in her favorite Italian cuss. "How could I *not* do this?"

~ ~ ~

Back in the mirror on party day, she jutted out her newly-40-year-old chin. *Okay, you stupid senseless fear. I will party like I mean it and fake you right out of your jockstrap. And, all my favorite friends are coming. That crazy Doc . . . who knows what he'll come up with next.*

~ ~ ~

Skywalker's steady hoofbeats as he crossed over Pearl Street brought her back to the present. It wasn't busy yet, eight-thirtyish, locals getting coffee and their papers. *I timed this right,* she thought. *There's a café here somewhere with good strong mochas—ah, there.* She tied Sky to a meter. "I *adore* you, big. I'll bring you a treat, an apple if I can." She finger-combed her hair and replaced the dusty Stetson, threw on Jordan's shirt, and strolled into the café as if this were everyday fare for a morning out on the town. *Yum, it's like I can taste that coffee just by inhaling the exquisite scents in here.*

At a table near the door sat a former client, Bill Driver, squinting under his Stetson, smiling broadly at the sight of her. "Well good *mawnin'*, Miss Jillian. That's a fine mount you've got there, a *real* fine boy. Have you met my wife Lisa?" He gestured toward the attractive trim woman beside him.

"Morning, Lisa, nice meeting you." Jillian smiled, reaching out a hand to Lisa. *Such good work Bill did in therapy. He got right to it. We worked well together – it was that quality work that keeps us both on the edge of our chairs.* "Hey-yy, Bill. What a treat to run into you. Do you guys ride then?" going for the impersonal topic of horses.

Lisa spoke quietly in a cigarette rasp of a voice. *Streaked hair, expensive shirt.* "Yes, we used to keep horses, but not anymore. Too much wear and tear on the old bones. After I broke my arm . . ." she cut off a bite of omelet and gestured with her forkful. "Good breakfasts here. Great coffee. Our favorite breakfast spot."

Definitely a bit of an edge. Doesn't smile over-much, Jillian observed. *Bet she could bite.*

Jillian nodded. "Yeah, it *is* tough on the body. But I can't imagine life without a good horse pal like Skywalker there. A real gentleman." She tugged her shirt down, thought of explaining why she was dressed like this and decided not to get into it. *No defense needed. I'm on my own time and this **is** bolder Boulder, dammit.*

"Well, truly a pleasure seeing you guys. Guess I'll go round up a coffee and an apple like I promised my boy. You guys have a fine weekend." She strode to the counter, boot heels thudding so she rose up on the balls of her feet. A coffee and an apple and she was back out with Sky, leaning into his smooth sweet-smelling neck. "Coffee's just right, bud. How's your apple?"

He chomped, content, head close in to her. "I been lovin' you a lo-ong time, boy," she crooned. He nudged her shoulder with his muzzle and munched on. *You understand everything, you wonderhorse, you princely being.*

She sipped the invigorating coffee and reflected on the work with Bill. He was w*ell motivated, quick and smart, went right after it. From the relaxed look of him now, maybe the litigation is settled. I sure hope so. Good man.*

The screen door opened and banged shut. Lisa walked over to stroke Sky's forelocks, lips in a straight line. "Hey big guy. You're a handsome one." Sky raised his head, giving her a once-over, crunching his apple evenly. She spoke in a low tone with a southern drawl now. "So, Jillian.

Seemed you helped Bill sort things out a while back. Maybe therapy actually works sometimes."

Whoa. There's a chomp. Don't bite on that bait, girl. Now where'd I hear that? Grandma Corbett I'll bet. "Well thank you, Lisa. It was a real pleasure working with Bill. He dove right into the deep end. Gotta admire that kind of courage, willingness."

"Yes, he's got guts, I'll say that. Well, I just wanted to get my horse fix from this big guy. I miss these guys. Y'all have a nice weekend."

Jillian climbed on and they walked slowly home in the warming spring sun. "I think that's the sweetest wager you and I ever made, Sky buddy. Worth a few nervous Nelly moments. We should talk to our agents about taking this show on the road." She tucked her shirt back in the pack to play fair to the bet. Doc could be around any corner and he wouldn't hesitate to jump out of his truck and yell "Foul!", pointing accusingly. She chuckled at the sight.

They ambled up the ranch driveway, Skywalker anticipating the oats he knew he'd earned. He whinnied 'I'm back' to his buddy in the pasture and got a prompt response, quickening him into a trot. She reined him in to cool him, running her hand firmly down his neck. "Easy, pal, you'll be there in plenty of time for lunch. We did good out there this morning so chill on your laurels."

The screen door slammed behind Jordan, startling horse and rider. Jillian met his eyes and held. Tall and broad-shouldered with graying pony-tail, ice-blue eyes, leaning on the post. "Hey *wild*-woman. What's that string of pick-ups behind you?" He squinted in the sun, territorial scowl at the imaginary lineup.

"Bus-ted. I tried to tell them you were home so it was a no-go today but . . ." batting her eyes.

"Well then, if that pretty butt is mine for today, get on in here and let's see what trouble it can get into." Jordan fingered his mustache seductively.

"You heard him, horse. Move it." *An-tic-i-pa-tion*, she hummed. *It's makin' me cra-zee.* She whistled as she toweled and brushed Sky down, gave him his oats and walked him out to pasture. She sauntered into the kitchen with a half-smirk. "Not that I'm in a hurry, but you look *good* to-*day*. And I'm feelin' rich and sassy, so c'mere, Studly," unhooking her Bikini top.

As they rounded up their delicious afternooner, she watched Jordan lay back to light a smoke. *God I never get tired of this slow build-up loving. It's somehow new every time. Most times anyway.* She stroked his chest, letting the graying curls slide through her fingers.

"You happy, baby?" she purred.

He closed his eyes. "Whadayou think?" He tapped his ash.

"Mmm-m. Sweet. Oh man, Jord, I earned us those meals with my cold sweat out there. Pushed me to the moon to let it all hang out before God and all the people, but I gotta admit after a while it got kinda fun. All those rubberneckers – oh, and I saw a favorite old client at a coffee shack. He seemed in a good place after . . ." *Check the client confidentiality,* she warned herself. *This is a small town.* "Anyway, looks like it's behind him now." She took in his tight neck muscles. "So. Now you talk, Sweets."

He snuffed out his smoke and turned to cup her shoulder in a big calloused hand, kneading like she liked, eyes fixed on hers. "Shit, babe, it ain't getting easier to keep all those trucks movin' with gas prices soaring and insurance a nightmare. And everybody broke in this sumphole economy so nothin's movin'. Sober drivers like the dinosaur. Like I always said to Dad, 'No clue how you kept this outfit goin' all those years. Mom too when she took over for him. What, rubber bands? Duct tape'?" He dropped his voice an octave to mimic his dad's deep drawl. "Don' know either, boy, but it's your headache now and I don't miss it a DAMN bit'."

Jillian snickered, loving his wit and hating his daily grind. She massaged his neck until he purred, stretching the muscles out gently, firmly. "Here? Or more there?"

"Right there. That's better. Now I get why there's a line-up of trucks out there."

"Savin' all my lovin' for you," she sang, and slid out to the shower.

Chapter 2

Sister talk

"Callie-Callie-Call-eee. What's happenin', sis?" Jillian sang into the phone, visualizing Callie in her perennial pose with leg in air, rotating that clubfoot with a strap. *"Nemesis," she's been calling it lately, partly because she just likes the sibilant sound, and maybe to objectify it, like it's an attachment **to** her but not **of** her. And I **know** she's wearing raspberry and lime in some combo, tank top, clam diggers, pony tail and that toughgirl grin. I so love her very bones!*

"Hmm. Usual frickin' funny-farmsville," Callie moaned. Her voice sounded breathy to her sister of the perceptive ears. "Lacey has found herself another weirdo boyfriend. That girl is gonna self-destruct one of these days and I'm gonna fall through the chasm after her. If she doesn't shove me in head first. Have you thanked God yet today that you guys don't have kids?"

Jillian affirmed, "Daily. We never *were* cut out for it. I love yours to death but . . . so tell me more, Sissie."

Callie had learned endurance from her turned foot at birth. "Aghh – if I tell you what's really going on, you'll bust on me. How about you just listen while I bitch for one minute? Make it a half minute." She pulled her foot straight with the strap and winced. "*Shit* that hurts. Okay. Your turn first. Half minute bitch rant and then my turn."

"God you're tough, girl. So – are you ready for this? This can count as my rant but you're gonna split a gut. I rode Sky into town like Doc dared me, right? Your shy sister dressed like a gypsy ho in bikini? And on my professional turf yet. God that's guts ball for me. Got the stretch marks on my soul to prove it."

They shared a round of high-pitched hilarity. Callie gasped out, "Good one, J. I love it when it's *you* on the rack. Yee-hah!"

"Oh *really*. Bitch," Jillian snorted. "But that Doc knows where to land one, right? I was sweating bullets out there." Jillian loved a laugh at herself. *It's cathartic somehow, releasing, especially the sweet rear-view-mirror play-by-play with my Callie. That's double the mileage.*

"Good on you – that took guts and when you need 'em, you got 'em. But Jillie – why'd you do it, for real? What were you thinking? And that counts as a bitch rant – a bitch in a good mood for once," and they cackled all over again. Callie had a way of boring down for the core of things that Jillian appreciated. *Feels like she knows where to scratch an itch I don't even know I got.*

Jillian gave the question its due for a few beats. "Well. I think because it was Doc and I know he digs me and Sky too. He knew where to aim the challenge – my big fortieth calling for new turf to explore, a hard shove out of my comfort zone, and to see what a true prince Sky is in one more way. *And* not the least because Doc loves to crow about his wife's cooking," scratching her scalp.

Callie lowered her voice. "Lacey is handing me one of those yucko soul-stretchers as we speak. God. Do parents actually live through these teen years *ever*?"

"It's only lethal when they're dumb enough to pick it up, sis. What's the latest?" *Careful, Ms. Shrink. Stay in your own back yard unless invited in.*

Too late. "Can you just listen and not therapoke me just *once*, Jillian, damnit?" Callie snapped. "I'm not your damn client. I'm your *sister*. Jeez but that gets old. How many times have we had this stupid loop of a conversation?"

Long silence. Callie spoke first. "Sorry, Jill. Just share with me like sisters, okay? You're not on the clock and I am *not* paying for your damn professional services. I mean, your questions are good but -"

"No, *I'm* sorry. Ears, not mouth. I'll be good, sis. I was out of line. Shoot." Jillian massaged her inner thighs where the saddle had pinched her. *No wonder I love bareback. These welts are gonna turn all the colors of the rainbow.*

Silence. "OK. It's ancient history." Closer to the phone now. "So she's dating another older guy. This one's nineteen and actually employed. That's a step up in the trail of losers."

"Is she coming to you to talk?" Jillian sucked in her gut to a count of ten to help zip her lips while tightening her belly.

"Yeah right. She's ditching me as fast as she can. Telling me a whole lot of nada, or lies." Callie started to whine but checked it, unwilling to give Jillian the satisfaction.

"Sounds like you're letting it play out as it will. That's so smart. I truly admire your level head, sis, and you *know* I mean that. Wish Mom were as smart as you about detaching. I mean, she's great and all, but she does like to mind our business at times. Kind of an old-fashioned way, you think? You're much clearer about boundaries."

"Thanks sis. Oops, she's home, gotta go. Call you tomorrow, ok?" Callie hung up and stared hard at her phone. *I hate it when she gives me that professional crap, but who else can I talk to this deep? She gets it because she listens and she certainly cares, I gotta give her that.* She grabbed her foot and pulled the toes straight in a stretch. *Reprogram, you bitches.*

~ ~ ~

"Lu-unch!" Jillian called to Jordan from the deck. She watched as he ambled over from the barn, noon-high sun on his tall frame. *Those shoulders get more stooped every time I look. God I feel helpless watching him worry.*

She closed her eyes and breathed in the smells of ground and leaves of the cottonwood. Big Daddy, they had called it since Jordan's parents lived here. It had some bare spots now, a limb ripped off by lightning, its bark thickly grooved, its new yellow shoots pimpled. *Thank you for your gift of shade and your shishing leaves and creaking limbs,* she silently blessed it. *Even though you shed like a damn collie in spring.*

Jordan flopped down at the picnic bench on the shaded deck with a goofy smile.

Jillian raised her eyebrows luridly and picked up her sandwich. "Your faves, baby. It pays to keep Mama satisfied."

"Now that you mention it, woman." He tipped his glass to her. "Think I'm as dumb as they say?" with a twisty face.

"How's the sammie, goofball?"

He took a bite and garbled a "Grrreat," out of the side of his mouth, wiping off the mayo with his knuckle. "So you want to mow this mess or muck out the barn?" swallowing his pickle. "Can I have your pickle? Pleease? You know you want me to have it," whining like a two-year-old.

"Good thing I don't like pickles, ya' big baby," she mimicked, forking it over. "I'll muck, you mow. Because you have a lovefest goin' with that precious mow-toy."

~ ~ ~

At the party she cozied up in a window seat with a favorite colleague, Tory Brainard, who was shaking her close-cropped curly dark head in gladness to see her dear friend. *God she's stunning,* Jillian noted. *Cameo beauty, that flawless skin and those delicate features.*

"Hey Jilliebelle. I been waiting for you, honey. You look fabuloso tonight," with a warm hug. "But Jillie I got sad news – God. Our neighbor – just when you think you know someone . . . shame about my neighbor Bill Driver? You ever know him and Lisa? They were horse people once upon a time."

"What shame? What're you talking about? I just ran ino them at a coffee shack this morning - " Jillian sucked in her breath. "What about him?"

11

Tory saw her angst and put a hand on her friend's arm. "I am *so* sorry to say, Jillie – Bill hung himself in his barn this afternoon. Ambulances and cops streaming all over the neighborhood. He – was he client or friend?"

"Shit. Oh God. Oh SHIT, Tory." Jillian covered her face with her hands. "Oh my GOD. He was a *client,* a really decent one. About six months ago. GOD! I just saw him this morning and met Lisa at a coffee shack. Look, I can't - I gotta get out of here, Tor."

Tory kneaded her shoulder. "I had a hunch, who knows why. I figured it was better you hear it from somebody close and not some damn news rag or the street. The story going around is he was trying to save the farm by gambling with Lisa's money. Jillie, there's no way you could have seen this coming, for sure not six months ago. I'm guessing he took a recent financial hit and on impulse, or desperation . . ."

"Look, let's do lunch or a hike next week, okay? I need to talk with you but right now I gotta go. And I'm glad it was you who told me, but . . ." Jillian hugged her hard and went off to find Jordan.

One look at her and he stood, reached out a hand to her shoulder and looked closely in her face. Time to roll. He made some excuse to the friend and to the host about a trucking crisis and they left. "Talk to me baby," he said in the truck, his hand kneading her thigh.

She stared straight ahead. "Oh God, Jord. This rips me up bad. He was such a good – did real good work – this opens a hole in my heart." Tears squeezed out. "He was such a cool guy, Jord. Wise, and just real and *good.* And to see him this morning after six months? That's just *wrong.* And why do I have this sickening feeling that I haven't heard the last of this? If his wife needs someone to blame – this is *the* worst kind of failure in a therapist's dread of flat-out failures." She shuddered, pressing her fingers to her eyes.

Big-sky indigo silence absorbed her pain as they rolled toward home. Crescent moon shone a peaceful pointed white. Jordan's big hand rested on her thigh all the way home. Stars slowly lit up their firefly lamps across the velvet backdrop.

Chapter 3

Funeral

Jillian drove across town to Bill Driver's funeral with a gnarling dread in her belly. *I need to show up to respect Bill and Lisa and the family but oh **God**. I hope Tory gets here – she said it looked doable. Sure would help to have her beside me. What in heaven's name do I say to Lisa?* She thought awhile. *I be honest. I tell her how much I respected Bill. Not much more I can say.*

She found the funeral parlor and parked, checked in the mirror. *Smart to skip the mascara which wouldn't survive my tears if they decide to make an appearance.* There was a crowd around the entrance where Lisa stood in black dress and veil. She took a long slow breath and willed herself to go talk to her.

Lisa watched her approach with steady gaze. As Jillian reached her, Lisa spun abruptly toward her companions, her back to Jillian.

*Yikes. Mrr-oww. I'll take that as a not-now-probably-not-ever gesture. Anyway what I need now is to be with Bill. Oh **please** be here, Tory.* Inside, she looked around the long rows of chairs where maybe thirty people bowed their heads in silence. *No Tory yet.* Now she could hear the soft snuffling sounds around the room. *That man had to be loved by lots of . . .* and her tears started. *Oh God, the casket's closed. That's* *so final. Figures, though. He must have looked rough. Better that we all remember the handsome smiling face.*

She chose a seat near the back and let her forehead rest on her fingertips, eyes closed in contemplation.

Now, Bill, man, are you here? It's so hard, incredibly hard, that you're truly – actually d-dead. I loved working with you. I valued you. There, I admit it, you were a favorite. I sometimes wondered if you were getting as much out of our time together as I was. Seemed a lot deeper than many folks can go and that's what made our work so engaging. What was so hideously wrong, man, so hopeless? She felt wet on her cheek and dabbed it with a tissue.

Feels like these tears are as much for me as for you – the release my body knows how to do. God, Bill, why? Lots of snuffling around the room now, like permission given by each other to let it all out.

So. Will you come find me on the other side, wherever, man? I need to talk to you one more time – got some big questions that you might know how to answer now. She sighed and let her torso sink. *So now, ride on with God, man. That's my first question when we meet up yonder – who is this God? Is He pissed that you, you know, took your own life? How does He or She or It look? Is It even a form that you can see? Touch, even? How does it communicate?*

Finally Lisa and her daughters entered and sat up front. There must have been seventy five people now crowding in and spilling out in the hallway. The service was tense and formal, as grim as Jillian had seen. *This minister couldn't have known Bill much. This is downright generic, doesn't even come close to resembling the guy I know. Knew. Go stuff your damn platitudes, buddy,* she flushed in sudden rage at this whole stupid charade. *Short-changing my man **now** in his **death**?*

*And what if **you** were bullshitting **me** like this poor stumbling fool? What if those tears covered the guile of a true gambling addiction? I've seen that kind of cover-up more than once. But no. You were gut-wrenching sobbing some days. You'd have to be a professional actor to pull that off. No. **No.** I'm not buying that.*

She focused on meditative breathing for several minutes, her mind far from this sad scene. Then . . . *God I hope this gets over soon. Hard to be agonizing and killer-boring in one service but this poor stand-in dude managed it. But maybe it's just me . . .*

Finally the closing hymn started its relief. Jillian waited for the room to clear so she could try again to express her regrets to Lisa. Maybe the service had softened the situation a notch. She stepped in when a space cleared around the three women. Lisa turned slowly toward her as if she'd been waiting for this. She glared through hooded eyes. Jillian caught the opening and closing of black-gloved fists in the corner of her eye.

"I'm so very sorry, Lisa. This is – so hard - " she mumbled.

"You did this," Lisa hissed in low tone. "You incompetent fake like all the other incompetent shrinks. He came to you for **help** and you **failed** him in the most final way possible. You therapists, all of you – you milk struggling people for a fat fee and do **nothing** to help. Well, you phony waste of time, I'll see that you never let a good man die in this town again. You *will* be hearing from my lawyer."

She spun away and stalked off on staccato beats, trailed by her black-clad daughters who glared at Jillian as they hustled to keep pace with their mother.

Jillian walked blindly to her car and somehow crammed her body inside and then crumpled over the steering wheel.

*Oh Jesus God in heaven. If you are anywhere in the vicinity, if you even exist, **show** me **please.*** She gulped air, stunned. *God what hatred. I have just lost every shred of dignity a therapist can lose. I did fail that poor guy – oh **God** . . .*

She drove to her office to cancel the day's clients, then slowly home to crawl into bed with a heating pad and a cup of chamomile tea. Her body felt like it wasn't there, like she was a raw clump of agonizing nerve. Somewhere in a blessed escape nap her mother called.

Damnit! I just wanted to escape awhile in sleep. She rallied for Sary. "Hey Mom."

"You sound rough, honey. Want to tell me what's going on? Or not?" Sary had failsafe radar about her girls in fair or foul weather.

"I'll call you after a bit, ok? I was sleepin'. . ." she murmured.

Several hours later Callie put a casserole and a salad in her refrigerator and padded softly upstairs. She peered around the corner.

Jillian heard and mumbled, "So. The wires were hot this afternoon? The professional worry wart?" She rolled over, yawned, patted the bed beside her.

"Yeah, bein' her mom self. We would expect maybe she'd turn into Jack the Ripper at a time like this?" Callie flopped beside Jillian and fished a stash of her sister's favorite Godiva chocolate out of her pack, holding it out temptingly.

"Will this oil your tongue? Because I know you, girlfriend. You got to get this shit sandwich moving so it won't fester."

Jillian smirked, chose a caramel and sea salt piece and fumbled with the wrapping. "Yeah, you do know and that's right on, damn ya'. So." She dropped her voice low. "Oiled by chocolate, Miss Jillian Shrinkydink began to spill her guts to her beloved sister."

They giggled like co-conspirators and Jillian haltingly began to unravel the grim details.

When she'd wound down, Callie said "Whoa. Grieving abandoned widow in full blown denial playing the blame game and you're it. Or is that just *my* take? What do *you* think?"

"Yeah, that's about it, seems to me. She needs a scapegoat for the horrible pain and I'm handy. And I was agonizing in my guilt so I didn't see her slide the hook in like you saw. Still, Cal, am I not a flippin' rooky incompetent douchebag? Damn you and your chocolate truth serum." She grabbed Callie's hand and kissed it. "Oh, soft. I love you." She pressed Callie's hand to her cheek.

The back door slammed. "What's up with you chicks, you loafin' around watchin' the soaps in the middle of the day?" Jordan yelled up the stairs.

"Hey hon. Callie's here nursing me after a slam-dunk at the funeral. C'mon up."

He ran up the stairs and ducked into the room, frowning. "Hey Cal."

Jillian saw dread in his blue eyes and paled. "What's wrong? Jord?"

"Sky's hurt."

Callie stood and quickly gathered her stuff. "Call you guys tomorrow. Holler if there's any news."

"Yeah, thanks a bunch, Sissie." Jillian threw on jeans and a shirt and ran down the stairs with Jordan close behind. "What happened? Where is he?"

"Looks like he reared up – snake, maybe, cougar, somethin' spooked 'im – and came down on a fencepost and broke his leg. He's lookin' bug-eyed scared out of his wits. In the pasture." They were sprinting now.

"You call Doc?" *This is hideous. Could anything worse . . . this miserable rotten no-good day . . .*

"Yeah, he's on his way."

"Shit, man. **Shit.** I love that boy so bad – what a day from hell. What frickin' else?" she yelled to the heavens.

Sky's head came up with a snort when he saw them. She cried out at the sight of him – his eyes fogged in pain, wire twisted on his leg which angled oddly below the knee. She gasped, then reached to hold his head close in to her body, kissing his muzzle, stroking his neck, tears streaming down her face. "My baby, my boy. We'll get you fixed up, big. Stay strong, buddy. Love you *so* much."

Doc's truck came flying down the lane in a cloud of dust. He ran over, medicine bag banging against his long legs, a frown on his craggy handsome face. "Hey guys. What's up big fella? Somethin' spook you out there?" He rubbed Sky's neck, then knelt to examine the break. After a minute he shook his head. "Nasty break. Let's lay him down off the leg so I can get a close look. It's gonna take all of us and then some. I'll get some acepromazine into him, that's a mild sedative, and in a minute you guys can ease him down against my back. Real slow and easy so nobody gets hurt. Got a blanket to put under him?"

Doc put the syringe together while Jillian ran for a blanket. Jordan held Sky's halter and stroked his cheek, crooning to him. "You are one steady dude, bud. Lord knows how stinkin' bad this hurts. You are my hero all over again, man. There now, bud. It'll get easier now," as Doc jabbed his flank. Sky flinched and then held steady, eyes wild with fear. Jillian ran up with the blanket and laid it out. Doc bent down, bracing forearms against thighs. Sky snorted and faltered, held a minute, then stumbled and closed his eyes. Jordan and Jillian eased him gently against Doc, who dropped onto his knees with the weight, then let Sky down on the blanket. Once down, Doc could slide out from under Sky without anything breaking.

"Phew. That's a whole lotta horse. Damn," and he stood and shook out his hands.

Sky lay still with wild eyes, snorting, breathing hard. He shook his head up and down, then his lids closed once, opened wide, then closed and held. Doc moved in to clean the wound and examine it more carefully.

"Fibula's smashed like I feared. That's gonna need a couple of pins. We can't do that here, Jord, he needs clean surgery. Colorado State University clinic at Fort Collins does good work with this kind of thing. When this dose wears off, I'll give him a local anesthetic for the pain and a leg brace to hold it in place and then we can winch him up and trailer him. Call now, Jillian. Here's the number – see how soon we can take him in. Should be twenty-four hour service."

Jillian ran to get her phone. Jordan asked the question he knew she was loath to ask. "Will he – um, ride again, Doc?"

"Prob'ly not, Jord. The running weight might be too hard on this – but he's a tough hombre. We'll wait see and keep giving him our very best. Never say never, man. Now let's go figure how we're gonna rig up a winch to get him up and on the trailer."

An hour later Jordan and Jillian were driving down to Denver with Sky loaded in the trailer, strapped under his belly to the sides to keep his weight off the leg. They sat close together and drifted off in their own thoughts. Jillian leaned against Jordan's shoulder and several miles later, fell asleep.

Chapter 4

Back at work

Jillian took the next day off, too foggy to work. She went to the hospital to visit Skywalker, loved on him awhile, and went on home to mope. She called Sary and filled her in, then sat with her over tea when Sary brought over some chocolate chips.

"Oh honey," she kept saying with a puzzled frown. "I'm so sorry. I feel so helpless. You don't deserve all this stuff."

"Thanks, Mom. Just your being here helps. Really. How's Daddy?" changing the subject.

Next day Jillian drove to her office for a full day of clients, worrying about Sky all pinned and screwed together. Next on her worry list was Jordan's news of the broken-down truck in Glenwood Springs, his increased smoking. Then there was Lisa Driver's threat to discredit her. That sent a flush of adrenalin through her gut.

A switchback in the road called her attention back to now and the beauty of huge red boulders contrasted with Colorado blue sky. *Whoa. It's so powerful, this landscape. That intense cerulean sky framing all these shades of green, aspen and pine, this pure clear air . . .*

And now the shift back to her meandering mind, cruising along with a tiny gratitude for this moment, this view, this day ahead. She popped in a Holly Near CD for upbeat licks. *I love that I love my work – and I do know how lucky that is. A lot of folks I know have grinding jobs they hate. Mine feels like my calling, like it's right where I'm supposed to be. Weird how right that feels. I see people's courage and beauty when they can't see it for the pain. However did I land in the catbird seat, sharing in people's naked soul questioning? Like Bill's, bless his soul. . .*

Around a bend – errrrgh! She screeched to a stop for a big mama elk and her baby standing unconcerned in the middle of the road. *Thank You, Whoever or Whatever. Whew. Thank you for that missed encounter.* She pondered on the serendipity of moments like that, encounters that could have been disastrous but were somehow avoided.

Sky's busted leg because of, what, a passing snake? A pack of coyotes or a cougar? Is it chance that Jordan is losing business or are we making bad decisions, or possibly being guided in another direction? The stock-hauling market is just drying up?

She got to the office and met her first client, a 40-something mom who was having an affair with her boss and feeling very guilty. "What keeps you going down this road despite the agonizing guilt? Great sex? Is he the love of your life?"

"The sex is okay," Carla the soft-spoken brunette admitted, rocking her palm back and forth. "And no, he's not the love of my life." She smoothed her skirt. "Good question, Jillian. Your questions help me figure my own way through things. Maybe it's that I'm pissed off at my husband who I still love for the boring non-conversation dinners, the soccer games mostly alone on the bench, the agony of watching him drink himself into oblivion most nights. I hate what my life has become! I need some connection *some*where. I know this isn't right but I don't want to disrupt the kids' lives by leaving him. My parents were divorced and that's no picnic." She was silent for several beats.

"Maybe I don't want anything that looks like my mom's life. She was so moody. Dad drank a lot. Maybe I'm trying to have my cake and eat it too."

"Have you heard of Al-Anon, for the friends and families of alcoholics? For the sheer comfort of knowing you're not alone with this miserable disease? People share honest tools to cope and even thrive with an active alcoholic in their lives. I've seen it work wonders, like AA does for the alcoholic who wants it. I know an alcoholic who watched her partner get healthy in Al-non and that ruined her drinking, which made sobriety look interesting, even possible for the first time." She lifted her eyebrows.

"A girlfriend at work told me about that. Maybe I'll check it out with her. She swears by it and she's in an alcohol-soaked marriage like mine."

Jillian noted in Carla's chart: 'Suggested Al-Anon. She might respond to the emotional/spiritual connection to fill the void of husband's drinking instead of current affair. Community could help her choose what works for her.'

Next clients were parents whose fifteen-year-old gay son came out to them after he was kicked out of school for fighting. "At least now we understand all the fighting this gentle soul has been doing. We had no idea how - or why - he was being bullied." Jillian noted: 'Martial arts for son? Son and dad? Mom doesn't look like she'd buy in now but maybe later if it provides bonding for dad and son.' For now Jillian listened carefully as they grieved what they were grappling with and encouraged their natural compassion.

Third hour. A fortyish black man, Charlie, whose gambling was overtaking his life. This one was a little too close to Bill Driver's story and hooked her for a few beats until she caught it. *Watch the countertransference, girl. Spend some time later meditating on the differences between him and Bill to clear your head.*

Lunch time. *Lemme see what Tory's up to – I love her straight feedback.* Tory was able to break free so they grabbed some take-out and went to a favorite lookout bluff. "How're you doing with Bill's death, pal?"

Jillian gave her a contorted smile. "Not great, Tory. It's hard to shake the guilt, and then I see Lisa coming after me with both guns blazing in a dream. Dream, hell – psycho nightmare. One of those recurring ones? A body hanging from a barn beam, boots turning slowly in the wind. God. And Jord's business is close to tanking, poor guy. The slump of those broad shoulders tears me up. Grandpa's got colon cancer. Anything more you want to dump on my doorstep?" She grimaced skyward. "This is what Callie and I call a bitch rant."

"**Shit**," they sang out in chorus, fist-bumping at life's bizarre twists.

"I'm just sayin', Tor. It wouldn't take a torrential wind to push me over a cliff these days. Every time I look at Sky and know we can't ever ride out again, it feels like my heart is being slowly squashed. And all these clients counting on me and I can't seem to shake off the crap like I used to."

She looked to Tory whose face was contorted with concern. "**SHEE-ITT!**" Tory screamed. "Good thing this is Boulder and everybody already knows we're all looney tunes. Look, Jillian - you **get** yourself to a hotsprings for a couple of days and soak this out of you. I mean it girlfriend. And massages. I don't want to come visit you in the funny farm. It's getting to you – your perspective sounds way off. I know *I* can't work like that – I gotta find my balance or I'm no good to others. I know I'm loud and pushy and you're the opposite but . . ."

Jillian thought about that, walking quietly. She understood the differences in their personalities too – she the introvert to Tory's extrovert. And yet - she walked on.

"Okay, you're right, Tory. I'm ain't-it-awfulling because it's too much. For *me*. Overwhelming. Maybe not for you or somebody else." Jillian's fingers went to her temples to press in, massaging in circles. "And Doc didn't actually say Sky would never ride again . . . I exaggerated that."

"That bugger fear again," Tory nodded. "That cripples me faster'n anything."

Back at the office Jillian was doing paperwork when a call came in.

"Jillian Nicholson," said a familiar husky voice. "This is Lisa Driver. You might want to check the paper today." Click.

Jillian thought to get a bracer drink of water before returning for two more client hours. She forced her mind to full attention on the people in front of her. One powerful woman spent the hour blaming her husband for all her many misfortunes, not recognizing responsibility for her part in it. Jillian intervened a couple of times judiciously but didn't get much traction. *She'll go home and think about this conversation, and maybe in the shower get an epiphany as she sometimes does.*

Next hour brought a depressed teenager, Anna, who wanted to be a musician but whose lawyer father was forcing her into a law career. *'Father narcicisstic'?* Jillian noted. *'Bring him in for mediation; empower Anna to confront him.'* She locked up the office, so drained she fumbled the lock, cussing it.

Driving home she stopped for a paper and stuffed it under the passenger seat out of temptation's reach until safely home. She screamed BITCH BITCH BITCH! at the windshield until her tonsils ached. Only one passing driver stared, making her finally laugh at the absurdity of it all.

Chapter 5

Changing course

The obituary laid out some facts about Bill Driver's life and sudden passing but gave no cause of death. The last sentence read, "Mr. Driver had been treated recently for anxiety and depression by a local clinician unsuccessfully."

She laid the paper down gently, leaned back in her chair, closed her eyes and faced forward into the wave.

Her first thought: *She stopped just short of defamation of character, thanks be to the threat of lawsuits and courts. If she could have pointed a large cosmic finger at my door by naming me, she surely would have.* She was staring into space when Jordan came through the door.

"Hey Wookie – *oh* shitsky." One glance at her mascara-streaked face sent him off to the kitchen to return with wine and cheese with crackers. "Emergency supplies coming right up. Spill it, Wook."

She roused for him as best she could. "How was your day, my darling?" drowsily. "All of it, the poop and the pretty. Nice alliteration, huh?"

"You don't look like you want the full bore. You look like the shit truck just dumped a hefty load in the front yard." He drummed his fingers on his knees.

"But I do. I do. Lay it on me. We'll get to my shit all too soon, sweets."

She sat up for whatever was coming and took a sip of wine. "Nice," with a little tilt of her glass. She watched the dark burgundy liquid swirl around in the glass reflecting the soft light of the lamp.

"That rig in Glenwood Springs, remember?" he mumbled.

She closed her eyes and nodded, then cut off slides of cheese and placed it on crackers.

In that choked voice she knew too well, "Gonna take eight grand to fix. Needs a transmission, ball joints and a rear axle. I have about two, two fifty maybe. I can't wrangle that kind of dough now. I'll have to sell it for scrap. The trailer's not too bad; it should bring a fair price but not enough to replace the cab. And I can't cover the western slope without that rig. No wonder it's the first truck to go – it gets worked harder than all the rest together because that's the only part of the state stock is movin'."

Jillian felt his news hit her like an eight ball in the solar plexus. The broken down truck was bad, irreplaceable for the business in fact. But Jordan's suffering devastated her and she knew she had no power to fix it. *Shit! I HATE that I'm so frickin' helpless and I love him so much.*

Hot tears started somewhere behind her eyes, spilling down her cheeks. Jordan saw and understood, reaching for her hand. His chin sank to his chest. They sat in the slowly darkening silence of dusk without the least possibility in sight.

Finally in what felt like an hour later, Jillian handed him the newspaper article. He read it slowly, shaking his head once, then dropped it in his lap. "Helluva malicious note to end a guy's life on. She must have hated him pretty bad. Or herself. She all but named you as The Unhelpful Therapist."

Jillian stared at him. That Lisa hated herself had not occurred to her.

~ ~ ~

In the weeks following, Jillian found herself daydreaming as clients talked, drifting in and out of topic, willing herself back to the present. She double-booked clients twice and admitted her mistake, eating the fee. Once she felt her eyelids droop in a late-afternoon session with a long-winded man. The client called her on it and she apologized. They got through it all right, but her self-criticism droned on mercilessly. She well knew the symptoms of depression.

Her monthly supervision session was scheduled for that Thursday. "I'm losin' it, Dr. Jake," she confessed to her adviser. "I'm not tracking people like I usually do naturally. I'm distracted. I even double-booked clients *twice* this week. And I was nodding out in a session and the guy caught it and called me out. Jeez. Some therapist. *I* wouldn't want me for a therapist. I'd sense that lack of caring presence and shut down so fast . . ."

"How do you handle that, when you double-book? I mean ethically. Which we all do once in a while, you know," tamping his pipe ashes and peering over his half-glasses. Graying wispy blond, mustached, dapper, with sharp ears and quick smile. She trusted him, had been working with him for a couple of years. He modeled thoughtful listening and she thirstily absorbed it.

Fair question about my ethics. "I just eat the fee. Does that sound right?"

Dr. Jake nodded, looking out the window. "Yeah, me too. So – it sounds like you're working on a classic case of burnout, Jillian. How about taking a couple of weeks off to re-calibrate? Get out of Dodge. This is a normal hazard of the trade, girl. It's intense work, listening to human dilemmas all day long, and when you throw in some crap from home, and you've got energy drainage or worse, depression, which it sounds like you're in - too much on your plate." He rubbed his hands and steepled them to his lips.

"Take a vacation recently? Yeah, I thought not," with a wry smile. "Why not trust the burnout your radar is providing and follow it down? There are important new possibilities in this kind of turn in the road." He looked the soul of compassion with his soft brown eyes and wild eyebrows.

She felt the clarity of his understanding, which ramped down her anxiety. In soft voice, palms together unconsciously mimicking his, "I hear you and I know you're right. I'm not having any fun. But we might just lose the farm so there ain't much slack here."

"Ahh – more stress. So there couldn't be a better time to make a change, right? Look, Jillian, I know how you love the place and Skywalker but think about it – it's a ranch. It's replaceable. You aren't. You're in need of change that comes from your gut, your deep inside." He pulled his belly in with a breath. "I happen to know of a real good therapists' R and R clinic for times like these and folks like us. It's a few hours' drive across the Kansas border. Take a look at their website." He scribbled an address on a notepad and handed it to her.

"Really, Dr. Jake? *This* is *nec*essary? I mean – I believe you but the timing . . ."

"Which is why now, Jillian. The stressors are piling on you, girl, and your life and your clients' lives matter *too* much to fool around. Don't get up in your ego here and defend yourself – and don't waste your breath bullshitting a bullshitter, 'cause I've been there. Do what *you* need to do to take care of *your*self because nobody else can do that kind of surgery *but* you and higher wisdom beyond you. Just like you'd be telling a client about now. Or me, if you'd been supervising me when I lost it and needed a break. I tried booze but didn't find the truth I was searching for in a bottle of bourbon," he raised an ironic eyebrow.

"Man, Dr. Jake. I know I can't see clearly when I'm teetering on the cliff here but – that helps, to know you've been there. Thanks for that honesty, it levels the playing field. Lots of noise in my head. I read once – maybe Hafiz, the Persian 13th century poet? 'Noise is a cruel ruler.'"

"Attaboy, girl. Know when to fold 'em, like the song says. Surrender just before you get bludgeoned," he grinned and rubbed his eyebrow with two fingers. "Because it's now, or it will get worse. Somethin's trying to get your attention. And it will."

She drove home ruminating on Jordan's possible reactions, imagining all manner of resistance. She was least prepared for the response he came up with.

When she put dinner on the table and sat down, he lit the candles and said, "I've been watching you, woman. It's my job, remember? Life mates?" wagging a forefinger from his head to hers. "Dr. Jake's right. It's just too much shit on you and it's pointing at some kind of change, I sure don't know what but . . ." He cleared his throat. "The timing sucks, is all, which is a big part of what you're thinkin'. But these trucks ain't your problem so you do what you need to for you. I'll figure somethin' out – I ain't gonna watch *you* sink with this shipwreck. Besides, insurance should help with this. They must pay for SOMEthin', the slimy sharks." He raised his wineglass to her.

"You're . . . amazing. I don't know where you get such brass balls but - " She leaned in to kiss his nose. "I need a think with the pasture-dweller out there." She finished her meal and walked out to the pasture in the deep dusk. Sky limped right over. "Hey big. How's your day goin'? You got some wisdom to share for two bits?"

He dropped his muzzle against her belly, nickering and sniffing her pockets. She held his head close and warm, reached up to stroke his ears absently. They stood leaning there together, breathing together.

"I feel you, buddy. Primal. Pure love like I feel for you. And that's your wisdom for me. Don't know what I'm gonna do yet but – here's that carrot two bits you're rooting for, you hulk of an opportunist."

Chapter 6

Breakdown - July

By the end of the month, Jillian knew she had slid further down the chute of ineffective to bordering incompetent. Burnout and anxious about it. She sat through sessions willing herself to pay attention but for the first she could remember, she dreaded going to work. She felt wiped out at the end of the work day, and Jordan noticed she was losing weight, hardly eating and exercising only when she had no excuse. Callie called it straight – depression. "This ain't you, sis. The fire's gone out of you. Draggin' your furrows shut behind you, like Grandma Tanner used to say."

Jordan looked in her eyes with a concerned face and said, "I'm worried for you and that's a first *ever*. And it doesn't feel good, Wookie."

"You know we can't afford a break, hon." She felt the walls closing in.

"We can't afford *not*," he said in that choked voice of worry.

Her mother brought ginger cookies and a wrinkled forehead. "You know I don't say *this* often. DO something, girl. Get outa town. I'm not kidding you."

Callie said, "You're smarter than this, ya' dumb shit."

Jillian finally said "**Uncle** already!" and made her call to the clinic called St. Luke's in Kansas. She thought the name boded well. "St. Luke, wasn't he Jesus' doctor friend?" she asked the intake person, who assured her, "None other, dearie," in cheery British tones.

"At least they can take me quickly. It has to be *now* or I'll lose my nerve," she told Jordan. "***God*** but I'm busted."

"I like that it's called St. Luke's," he said, stroking an imaginary Freudian goatee. "Ve vill get your shpiritual head schrewed back on schtraight, Missus." They chuckled and snuggled, relieved. Finally some movement toward the normal they had taken for granted for a lot of sweet years.

"Jillie, I told the boys what's happening. Told them to update their resumes. To a man they said, 'Not happenin', boss. Not yet anyway'. Rad said, 'when that honky-assed sheriff knocks at my rusty old door with a 'viction paper in 'is hand.'"

"Wow, hon. They're the best, those loyal dudes. I love how guys *act* their love out and they *do* love *you*." She felt her lower lip quiver like a child's and covered with a laugh. "What a blubber baby I'm turning into."

"Crying is good for you, ain't that what you preach? Tears are natural re*leas*ers and *de*toxers," he mimicked in falsetto, wagging his head.

"Yeah but that doesn't mean I can *do* as I say." She made a self-deprecating face and went off to pack.

~ ~ ~

Sunday morning. Jillian hugged Sky and Jordan and headed out the lane bound for Kansas. *Two weeks – damn. Haven't had this kind of time away from home and work in, what, ten years? This place sounds peaceable, a restored inn. Good thing insurance is covering this or there'd be no way. My worst part so far was telling my clients. I felt so weak, so pathetic and vulnerable. Why would they keep believing in me? And yet only one switched over, and to Tory who will be a better fit for her I think.* She switched from radio to CD and stuck in her favorite, the Beatles' *Let It Be*, letting the sound pound its drumbeat through her, singing along, gripping the steering wheel as if poised for flight.

30

Plenty of open road ahead for a mind drift. I miss you already, Jordo. And Sky. She sent a mind-message to Jordan: *be extra good to my baby, honey. God he is one courageous champion. And to yourself, my angel man with the droopy shoulders and the what's-your-hurry lovin'.*

She thought of all she was leaving behind that mattered. *And please, Whoever You are, if You are, watch over those guys while I'm gone,* and *Grandpa too.* She envisioned him lying in his hospital bed, ashen and fading. *Grandpa, stay strong on your journey, buddy. We all love you, you ornery old goat. You're part of us. Wish me and Cal had got to know you more but you were off working all the time. Your dumb choice. And Dad – I'm sorry for your loss, and Grandma. I love you bundles, my sweets. And Mama.*

She watched her mind drift through years of family dinners with Grandpa Clark and Grandma Corbett, especially the Thanksgiving dinner when he blustered and barked at Dad so bad. *Was I the only one who saw his soft teddy-bear heart? Grandma must see it or she'd have decked him, as fun as she was. Callie hid behind me when he was around, and Mom usually had a spare hand draped somewhere on Dad. And yet they're close, Dad and him – only son and all.* She breathed into the smile inside her mouth for her dad's loyalty and drove on singing *"let it be-e, let it be-e-e."*

Next in the lineup came an image of Bill Driver – their good work together, on the edge of their chairs, probing the difficult facts and emotions of the embezzlement and betrayal by his cousin whom he had trusted with their families' welfare. She blinked to shut it out.

Mid-afternoon she pulled into the clinic parking lot. She hauled her bags inside to the front desk where a hefty peach-skinned receptionist called out her name. "Jillian Nicholson from beautiful Boulder, Colorado? Right on time. I'm Tracey-the-Brit. Cup of tea while I get some info from you?" indicating a seat beside her desk. "Just a minute, dear," and she waddled to the kitchen, stockings swishing.

Jillian looked around at the high ceilings and flowery sage green wallpaper. *Old make-yourself-to-home green,* she grimaced. *Hope this indicates they spend their money on staff salaries.*

"Here's your tea, sugar." She made some chatter about her swishing chubby legs, the weather, and anything else that moved or stayed still. Jillian relaxed a notch, her tense road muscles easing with the hot tea and Tracey's friendly chatter. She rubbed her stiff neck, handed over the paperwork and savored her tea with hands wrapped around the mug.

Tracey paused, leaning over the paperwork. "There's one thing, Jillian. You have a roommate – couldn't be helped on this short notice. I think she'll be – she'll make your stay a bit funner. *I* like her. Lemme know if it's, y' know, okay." She raised her eyebrows in the direction of Jillian's room. "Anything at all that you need, I'm your girl, and I'm all about comfort, lovey. I think you'll fit right in here, I do," and patted Jillian's knee.

"I could listen to you talk all day, Tracey. Love your accent. It was you I talked to last week then?"

Tracey grinned. "The very same, duckie."

She helped Jillian carry her bags down the hall to #112, opening the door with a soft "Hello?"

They looked in on a large dark-skinned woman, snapping black eyes staring back, untamed salt-and-pepper Afro, rocking by the window. "Well? Come on in, wha'cha waitin' for, an engraved invitation?" She threw back her head and let out a chortling belly-roll laugh. "Thanks, Miss Tracey-the-Brit. They call me Norrie back in Chicago. Jillian, right? From the mountains of Colorah-doe. Your bed's that one," pointing. "*If* you don't mind being by the door. I'll try not to keep you up with my snorin' or you have permission to sling a pillow at my head."

"Thanks, Tracey. Yeah I'm from Boulder, Norrie. Good to meet *you*." She took Norrie's hand, looked full in her eyes. "So tell me - what's it like here? Gimme the skinny." She dropped her bags and tried the bed. About right. She felt weariness begin to settle around her like a fog.

"You're tired. More ways than one, yeah? Kick back, girl. So. Let's see – how it is here. The food is pretty decent, plenty of fresh veggies and fruit, and the staff is mostly on it. They try to make a place for us to get to what we came for. No meds allowed – you know, head-meds." She tapped her forehead. "They don't push you but they set it up so

32

you can work on y'self when you ready. I'm an addictions counselah, recovering from *my* drug of choice – that would be crack cocaine, booze only if I gotta." She wrinkled her mouth. "Chicago south side. They give me a scholarship here because them crack addicts are workin' me *too* hahd. My boss called me Crispy Critter one day in a meetin' an' we both cracked up 'cuz we knew it was time. She found this place, thank God. I feel like I'm startin' to breathe again." That irrepressible cackle shot out again.

Jillian took to her right off. She fluffed the pillows and flopped back on the bed to swap stories until the dinner bell rang.

"Dindin," Norrie sang in a beautiful contralto. They went in laughing to a nourishing soup and salad meal. People were friendly enough but Jillian was too road-weary to make much social effort. "Tomorrow, tomorrow," she sang to Norrie.

As she climbed into bed that night she told Norrie, "I think I came to the right place at the right time, and you're making it so easy, girlfriend. I want more of that gorgeous voice. Oh, and don't blow it with your Olympic snoring."

"Welcome to the funny farm, girlfrien'." They giggled like middle school pals.

Jillian woke to a knock on the door and tiptoed to open it so not to disturb snoring Norrie. It was Tracey-the-Brit. "You're scheduled with your primary, Dr. Gomez, in a half hour. Hit it, girl. She doesn't like to be kept waiting. And Jillian. You just got lucky, she's the best here," she whispered. She lifted her chin a little toward Norrie, eyebrows raised. Jillian stuck her thumb up. Tracey shot her a wide smile.

Jillian jumped in the shower, making it to her first session with Dr. Idalia Gomez one minute late. "So sorry to keep you waiting, Dr. Gomez."

"Da nada. So we begin. What brings a lovely young soul like you to a place like this?" Dr. Gomez's warm black eyes invited her in. Fifty-ish, long wavy black hair clipped back from her attractive face and flowing down her back, magenta silk shirt over long denim skirt. *Mayan, maybe,* Jillian thought, *with those squarish high cheekbones. And like Tracey said, she gets right to it.*

Jillian settled into the chair she indicated, hands on thighs as she caught her breath, then willed her eyes to meet Dr. Gomez's direct gaze.

"So this is what it feels like to clients on this side of the desk. Intimidating, kind of naked. So – I've lost my compass, Dr. Gomez. I can't focus, I cry a lot, unusual for me. Or I'm anxious, also new for me. I'm detached from my work which I love – no, lemme get honest. I'm burnt out." She watched Dr. Gomez scribble on a yellow pad.

"Yes, this is usually a last-ditch stand resort," Dr. Gomez agreed, laughing. "So – causes for this now? Any events, special personal factors?" Dr. Gomez had a no-nonsense, friendly energy that made Jillian feel safe, like Norrie said.

She's wasting no time. Good because I've got only two weeks to figure my life out. "Lots of things," Jillian said, mentally going down the list. "My horse – a very brave special guy – busted his leg on a fence and we probably can't ever ride again. I've ridden all my life and he's the bravest animal I've – hmmh." Tears leaked down her cheeks. "My husband's third-generation livestock trucking business is going south. Nobody's shipping stock in this slow economy. My grandpa is dying and it's hard on my dad and mom." She pressed her temples.

"Okay, I'm with you so far. Is there one that pushed you over the edge or is it the combination of all these stressors?" Dr. Gomez asked, scribbling fast.

"Yeah there is one. That other stuff's actually more background noise." Jillian paused, palms on thighs, and took a shaking breath. "It's *really* hard to come here, to admit defeat, you know? I should be home helping Jordan – that's my husband – keep our heads afloat, helping Mom and Dad with Grandpa, seeing more clients to fill the money drain. Aghh." She folded her arms over her chest and reached for a tissue.

"About six months ago I finished working with a client – Bill – who'd been embezzled by his partner, his cousin, in his investments company. Bill was good to work with, you know, dove in to learn why this big loss had happened and what his part was. I hadn't seen him until a couple of weeks ago. I rode Skywalker – that's my horse – into town on a birthday dare and". . . she choked up again. "Ma-an these tears . . .

He looked good, seemed in good spirits, introduced me to his wife. All looked fine."

Dr. Gomez was writing and nodding, absorbing it. "And?"

"That night I was at a party with a close friend who told me" - she paused to breathe, thumbs on cheekbones and fingers on eyebrows - "that he hung himself in his barn that afternoon. Oh God," she blurted, hands covering her face. "I have nightmares of a body hanging in a barn, boots turning slowly. *God*."

"Aww, that's tough. And good releasing tears, Jillian. And good work that you got right to it, no wasting time. The sooner you dive into the deep end of this, the sooner you'll sort it out and heal it. I know you know that. No-nonsense work, like with your client Bill." She spoke softly in that matter-of-fact tone that gave Jillian confidence to proceed.

Jillian slid her palms together back and forth slowly. *She gets me. Sweet. Maybe I'll be able to dive down into this chasm with her guidance. OK, take a baby step, girlfriend.* "But because I *missed* that he was a gambler, didn't know it, now he's *dead* and it feels like it's partly my fault though I know it's not. And his wife wants to blame me, discredit me . . . she wants blood."

Dr. Gomez put her notes down. "Jillian. You think you are responsible for his death six months after finishing your work with him? Have you considered how much changes for any of us in six weeks, much less months?" She let that question hang in mid-air.

"And – this seems a good time to fill you in on what we do here, dear. We *do* what you have driven all this way for, you and your colleagues here, sharp therapists with fine practices, some quite famous. This need for re-calibration is built right into the work, Jillian, and I admire you for admitting your stuff early and getting the help it takes for you to go back and do better, clearer work – if that's what you choose for your future. I see you surrendering to this now so you can recharge. That takes guts *and* good resources. Don't judge this or yourself, use it. This work is for smart healers who're working too hard and caring too much, Jillian. We hope you'll learn here how to work smarter and less hard. It comes naturally as you deepen in your understanding of self."

A lovely cadence of Spanish in her soft speech – I like her a lot. It felt to Jillian like a long lapse until she murmured, "Thank you. I can work with that, Dr. Gomez. When do we meet again?"

"This time Monday-Wednesday-Friday. And Jillian, I have a good feeling about you getting what you need from this. You've made a fine start. I sense good instincts in you," smiling warmly.

Back in her room. Norrie was elsewhere. She brought her journal to her unmade bed to cozy in and write. *Dr. Gomez is one bright chick with a fine pair of ears. I can dive into this – this is my chance. Could be my only chance. Dark night of the soul time, maybe, but I can't know how tough it will get, only so far so good. Norrie's here for this same purpose and she's anything but a loser. So shut your stupid yap, fear.*

Okay. One issue at a time. So we lose the ranch/our home/Jordan's livelihood. Then where? Where will Sky go and who will love him like I do? No. Can't happen. And we living in some cramped crummy condo with no view of the Flatirons? And what would Jordo do – he's never worked anywhere else. He'll have to retrain and where's that money coming from? And to do what? She watched her mind spin, barely contained, waiting to jump the track into terror as soon as she was not looking.

OK. First layer – this bottomless grief. For Bill Driver, for Sky. Grandpa Clark. For the farm. For Dad's loss. That'd finish me if I lost my folks, my sis. And next – Lisa Driver's threat to my practice. Creeping cortisol flush in my belly every time I think of her, like poison oozing through my guts. I hate that feeling – like a pool of yucko shame and panic. Like I'm incompetent and I deserve this. And the whole town looking on. Impostor, fake, Lisa called me. How will the vulnerable people I treat feel when word gets around? Their trusted guide a hopeless loser who's crashed and is burning. No, wait, they know about this because I told them. God what a bottomed-out shit-storm, she wrote in large letters.

This is the work. I'll take this to Dr Gomez each meeting and keep track in this journal. She looked out the window. A breeze stirred the leaves of a maple tree – was that a little Mother Nature wave to me? She grabbed her journal and went to Tracey's desk to check out. "Go. Enjoy.

This isn't jail, Jillian. There's a little pond yonder in the woods where you might spot some wildlife if you go-o slo-oow."

Jillian winked and walked as slowly and mindfully as possible to the edge of the woods, taking in the scents of grasses, earth, the birdcalls, the distant hum of traffic, the flat terrain. *A little bit of heaven here.* A bullfrog croaked nearby, then splashed into the pond. *And bloody mosquitoes. Whap! Sweet that few of these critters have found their way to Boulder. Whap! Ma-nn! Glad you like it here so stay, darn your pesky hides.*

Chapter 7

Digging in

Jillian stopped on the path to breathe in the pungent smells and sounds of wood and water. *How can this be so hard, to just walk mindfully like that Buddhist monk Thay taught Callie and me what, two years ago? That retreat in Estes Park. Thich Nhat Hanh – yeah, that's his full name. What a peaceful man. We practiced his mindful walking for a while and really liked how relaxed it felt.*

Okay. She put her right foot down. *I wonder how many clients are reading Lisa Driver's news bulletin as I walk here, thinking it's me she's referring to.*

Left foot now. *Thinking, missy. Bring your mind back.*

Right foot. *Daddy? You okay, my love?*

Left foot. *I send you peace, Grandpa. Grandma.*

Right foot. *Shit. I can't do this so-simple task. I suck at mindful walking for God's sake. How hard can this be? When Thay – I believe that's "teacher" in Viet Namese – was modeling for us, Cal and I got it. Guess I'm just out of practice.*

Finally the edge of the pond. *Ah, a little bigger than Tracey figured, I'll bet an acre and a half. What a wonderful sanctuary – an old pond. A bit rank to the nostrils. Oh there, a weathered bench, mossy, inviting.*

She sat and let her legs flop wide, turning her neck on the rail for a hard massage. *Okay. Maybe I'm efforting here instead of simply walking. I just forgot how – my usual these days to be so critical. I wasn't brought up like that, so hard on myself. I remember being happy as a kid, riding out with Daddy, reading lots of stories with Mama, playing in the sandbox with Callie. Seems when baby Judd died – that was the turning point . . .*

She realized through a thought-fog that her cell phone was ringing. *Callie!* She answered eagerly. "Hey sports fan. How're they hangin'?" *Sweet connection – home. Sheesh but I love my little sissie.*

Callie's laugh was a short bleat. "Phew. Whatever they're giving you in that spa of yours, can you bring me some? You sound like a live human being for once."

"Yeah huh? So far it's a good place to do some deep work and that's giving me a dose of hope. Or else I'm just glad to hear your voice, my sweet sis. I'm already learning that I can't walk right – mindfully – like we learned on that Thich Nhat Hanh retreat, remember? Walking provides the perfect circus tent for the monkeys in my mind to cavort to their own calliope music. God."

They hooted together in high pitch.

Callie sighed. "Please. I still can't meditate. Unless I'm PMS'ing and then that's all I can do, more like moping. So really – it's working for you there? Tell me everything." Callie got her sister, zeroed right in to set the belaying pin.

"Yeah, Cal, thanks, ducky. You always know where to dowse. So. I got lucky with a cool roommate, a tough funny recovering addictions counselor from Chicago. And my shrink is really good, best one here they say. Dr. Gomez. Pretty Latina, forty five or so, with a sharp pair of ears on her. Group therapy starts tonight. So I'm gonna dive in because I'd be a true fool not to. I'm journaling to root out the snot and vomit that feels so jammed. Graphic enough for ya'?"

"Right. I'm packing now to come join your escapade. I don't bel*ieve* this kid I thought was my daughter but then the aliens – but you know all that old news. Hang in there, Wookie. You're tougher than you think and I've got the scratch marks to prove it."

"Big juicy hug, sissie." Jillian tucked the phone in her pocket. Something rustled at the edge of the bench. *Sounds small I hope.* A chipmunk darted across the path with a cheekful of something. Jillian inquired, "Hey, little fuzzy bit of Nature. How's *your* day goin'?" It turned to lock eyes with her. "Whoa. Taking a moment to check me out, yah pal? You like what you see? *You're* pretty cute with those stripey pajamas. Don't tempt me, I'm happily married."

He spun off into the woods.

She stood to slowly walk the path bordering the pond. *Now I'm doing it, mindful walking. It's not so hard, just a consciousness thing.* She stopped mid-step, left foot poised. *One, breathe, two . . .*

Oh. My. GOD. Is that the deal? This meshugeneh going round and round in my head – the fears, the shame, it's all just a choice of my **thoughts***? The story I'm telling about my life?* She looked around, saw no one, and let out a muffled war hoop. "Holy shit! *I'm* giving all this crap its only fuel!" She stood still, listening to the sounds in the woods.

"Go straight to hell, Lisa Driver. Grr-**RR**," she sneered like the cowardly lion.

~ ~ ~

First therapy group that night. The leader, short-cropped round Max-of-the-Facebush, introduced himself and the group. "This is Miss Jillian, y'all. How about you guys bring our new kid onto this merry-go-round with a few group guidelines, and then she can introduce herself to us? How 'bout you start, Miss Josie from Albuclosie? Albu*quer*que. Silly me."

Josie gave Max a down-her-nose look that brought a chuckle. "Happy you're here, Miss Jillian. R-E-S-P-E-C-T is the name of this ship. We work honestly on what brought us here and listen well to support each other. And you laugh at my jokes, especially the truly tacky ones," she declared with two thumbs up.

Jillian laughed with relief at the fun. She cleared her throat and looked to Max for permission to begin.

Max nodded. "All you, Miss Jillian."

She thanked Josie and Max for the welcome, shared a bit of background, then volunteered her afternoon's insight in a quivery voice. "Um, something new today. A chipmunk welcome? As goofy as it comes. This afternoon at the pond, a chipmunk turned and stared at me, and – uh, something kind of *opened* in me. I mean, I always half knew about Love or God or whatever you want to call that mystery, but until I hit the wall that got me here, I never **felt** it. It's like I knew **about** it but it didn't mean much. Abstract - " She tapped her head. "Up here. Not here," hand to her heart. She peered around the group for any inkling of understanding.

Max was nodding, his face registering clarity. Norrie was grinning and nodding, palms in the air, sending Jillian good vibes.

Jillian winked to Norrie and drew a long shaky inhale. "So – my story is, I was cruising along happily in happy childhood fantasyland. And then my baby brother Judd died and my safe little bubble burst. All Mom and them did was cry. I felt alone and so helpless. I loved her so *much* but I couldn't make her suffering stop. And I missed my Baby Judd so bad. So I played with my sister Callie a lot because – because Mama couldn't take care of her and Cal was so little and sad and had that clubfoot and all, and Grandma had her hands full with Mom. It gave me something that *I* could do, the big sister thing that was my role in the family. Guess that was when I became responsible to fix the entire universe. I was five. Truly horridly alone." She looked around at the group, her hands tightly grasped in front of her belly. "Wo. That was major. I mean, for me, not world-changing but . . ."

Max smiled crookedly at her self deprecation. "Huge and minuscule at once, right? Giant leap for mankind and a teeny baby step? But how can we work with clients if we don't understand the subtle path of growth from our own insides? If we ain't been there and done that?" He cleared his throat. "Say more about the way this feels transcendent, Jillian. And your chipmunk teacher."

"I mean I'm no theologian and I wasn't brought up religious, but I wonder about God a lot . . . who She or He is, how She works, if and when She works . . . it's all such mystery. I see this amazing *energy* when clients start to do some real work. Guess it's easy for us to see in other people but not in ourselves, right? They bring some issue in to therapy, something like a marital issue or a loss or crisis, say. And they don't know it but sometimes a trail of light seems to be around them, like a *glow*. God I feel so – vulnerable right now. Do you guys ever . . ." She looked around the faces and saw a couple of nods, enough to spur her on.

"Or with some, I can see their lives on a kind of center stage, and then over on this side stage, other issues and people show up to act out ways to help them break through to the new stuff. Or a health or financial crisis comes to wake them out of their usual humdrum world and I can see the crisis as a healing crisis. So why can't I see that perspective in my own crisis? I feel like a blithering basket case these days. I wouldn't let a client beat herself up like that." She felt raw, weird, and utterly naked before her peers who were strangers. *Oh my God. I can't believe I just said all that. What if they all think I'm completely whack-o?*

Max offered a warm smile of encouragement, tamping his mustache down with thumb and forefinger. "Wow, Jillian. You got right to work, girl, and named questions we all ask in a whole new voice. Your own. Beautiful, thank you. So – your chipmunk guru?"

Jillian felt a shaft of gratitude light up in her gut. *This guy respected my thoughts as they are and let them stand. Wow that felt empowering.*

"So this little busy guy out there in the woods was just being a chipmunk, not telling some high-falutin' story of His Wild Precious Life." She grinned and inched down in her seat to recover her wits, grateful for the laughter that followed. *Guess they understand my weird wit. That's a start.*

Josie stepped up with her crackling laughter, telling a great story about a rescue dog and laughing with shaking belly. She had a charm all her own that entranced Jillian.

At the break Jillian and Josie stayed in their chairs while the others went for coffee or water or fresh air or the potty. Jillian said, "You remind me of my mama, a poet and an earthy farm girl." She searched through her phone for a shot of Sary. "See what I mean? That wise face?"

Josie examined the photo with real interest. "Yeah, but is she Jewish?" she asked, holding it closer. "I guess one can be wise even if they're not Jewish. But it's rare, very rare. They put one in a museum in Ipsilanti and charge the people $4.50 to look at him." She nodded authoritatively, softly chuckling.

She turned a serious face toward Jillian. "You jumped in quicker and deeper than anyone here. That's courage, Jillian, and I bow to it. You got me thinking about Mystery – God as I call it. It's foundational to us Jews, and yet talking about religion doesn't play very well these days. But if I read you right, you're talking about Spirit, not religion, and that's inclusive enough for me. So I'll go along, so far. I'll keep you posted," as an afterthought.

Jillian nodded. "That's helpful, Miss Josie. Thank you."

Josie leaned toward her, hands on her knees. "I'm a writing teacher but first I'm a writer, a wife, and a mom to some interesting boys. Three of them. There were supposed to be two but one New Year's Eve – well, you know the rest of that line. So we say in private, Mike and I, 'two and change'. And that little one – *fulla* change." She shifted in her chair, rubbing her knees. "I'm working on my impossible career. No idea where to go from here. None. Choices are: retirement from teaching, which is being encouraged by my college at my age of ripeness. I love writing. I can sink my teeth into that. But I'm afraid I'll miss the fun of students and all their bizarre questions and piercings and false starts and wild hair and brilliance. And then there's the rocking-chair." She wrinkled her nose like a rabbit.

This woman is having too much fun, Jillian decided, grinning. *Well good then. This soul-search shit is tough. Why not find some outrageous laughing in the midst of all the doodoo?*

Back from break. A pale thin woman with a thick blond bun across the room said with a gravelly laugh, "Wish you'da been my English teacher, Miss Josie. School might have been fun instead of boring us all to smithereeens. Please go on. . ."

Josie nodded to acknowledge the praise. "Yeah, Marnie, they tried to put me to sleep too – but we faked 'em right out, didn't we now?" and the group exploded.

Josie looked at her hands, then rubbed them together. "Trouble is – I don't quite feel – I mean – I'm exhausted, truth be told. Thought if I came up here for R and R and got asked some good questions by some sharp shrinks – that's your job, y'all," sweeping her hand around, "I might be able to decide about heading out to pasture – maybe less like I was being shoved – I mean - "

Max sat straight up, hands on knees, looking in the faces around the circle, mustache twitching. "Well? You heard the woman. Whaddya got, you fine bunch of professional question-askers?"

All eyes avoided his as people sorted out their thoughts. He let the silence do its own work. Finally a forty-ish long-faced man named Al cleared his throat. *I can just see a pipe in his teeth and a wreath of smoke,* Jillian imagined. "What has teaching meant to you, Miss Josie?"

"Good question, Al," Josie smiled to him. "I love a good question. So. Giving it its due. It's meant daily intellectual challenge – all those preparations and misfires and baseline scores – pretty constant surprises. I LOVE surprises. And there are awful politics and stupid system decisions and wonderful people, a few awful ones, around me for twenty-five years. I have to imagine *not* being surrounded by lively minds and true hearts, lucky for me." She sat quiet for several beats.

Then, "Well. I guess I don't have to like it. Maybe there's a challenge as yet undiscovered." She folded her arms over her large chest. "I do love the next challenge," with a twinkle.

Jillian squirmed in the yearning to fix Josie's pain, a visceral creeping misery, like she wanted to massage Josie's heart. She bit her lip, hoping Max wouldn't notice and call her out.

"Miss Jillian. What's cookin'?"

He noticed. Damn his eyes. "Ma-nnn. I – ahh-hh – crap. I hate Josie's suffering – she's so flippin' cool – and I want to fix it and I know that's my codependence but – " She sniffled. Norrie walked the tissue box to her, touching her hand.

"Well. Guess this IS my shit, right here. I feel *real pain* for Josie and

I think it's my job to fix people and I failed with my client Bill D so I must suck at it. I failed with my mama after Judd died. I felt like a ghost slithering around the halls then, afraid to make a sound, afraid to smell funny or look weird or even be seen. Figured maybe if I was invisible, nothing worse could – God forbid *any*thing could get worse. The world had caved in, for God's sake." She snickered once at her little girl drama, then sat on her hands for a minute. "Wow. Poor little kid, caught up in all that illusion of power and nobody I could talk it out with because my best listener, my Mama, was the hurting one. I couldn't get anywhere near her without Grandma shushing me."

Long silence. Jillian found a shaft of gratitude in the silence. "Thanks, guys. And thanks, Miss Josie. Didn't mean to take your moment -"

"Nice work, Jillian," Max said softly.

Josie responded. "That's what's happenin' here, Jillian. You helped, you didn't take anything. That was brave. Shows me you care *and* that you got guts. That's support."

Chapter 8

Why am I here?

Jillian was in her room alone, snuggled in with tea and journal on a rainy Wednesday morning. *Why am I here?* she wrote. *No, I mean bigger than this clinic, this particular life. Here on Earth in this kind of a lifetime? If I can get a clue how huge the possibilities, that it might be different than what I've thought my whole life – untold universes, galaxies. I can't even imagine the vastness of all the life forms here on our one planet and beyond.* She stared out at the rain.

And then there's me, and whatever forces commingled to beget me? And why? For what purpose? I must matter or I wouldn't have been summoned and knit together in my mother's womb, as the Psalm says. And why did Baby Judd come and go so quick? Why was Callie born with a clubfoot?

She stared off into middle distance, chewing on her pen.

Even I can't argue with Is-ness, with what clearly exists. And I ***am***, *so there's the fact. Something somewhere thought I might just be a good idea. So it whomped me up with ingredients like cosmic dust and nitrogen and genetics from semen and egg and somebody's leftover tooth enamel. Am I living it as You intended, God, Whoever You are that stitched me up?* She paused, her eye caught by a huge yellow monarch butterfly. *And* *why didn't Judd get to live his life out? Was that the plan, that he should be born just to die?*

*Does that monarch butterfly out there know my answers? Then why doesn't the smart-ass tell **me**?* She watched it for the sheer joy and beauty of it until it flew off and she smiled. *Just kidding, buddy. Sweet day to you. Do you even have an ass?*

Back to you, Father or Mother God. May I call you Goddie, like Daddy to my inner kid, who I guess knows you. You ARE, to her. It's my logical mind that trips over every mouse turd it encounters! An irrepressible laugh ripped out of her at that.

Okay. If I am made of the same elements as the stars, as Einstein said, then the Source of all matter had or has a plan and I must be included in that. So I am a part of divinity. I read in the Bible once that Jesus said he came to show us that he was no different from us, made in Love and that we are too. If that's true then I am part of Divinity, whatever that means. Skywalker is divine – that's no mystery. He's supernatural. And Jord and me making love – takes us beyond this world. And when I work with clients, sometimes we get to such amazing places – I know it's real but I sure have no words for it. More tea and a butt scratch.

*I remember like it is happening now how desperate I felt when Judd died, how I longed to comfort Mom and Callie and Daddy. It was like a **thirst**. I tried so hard to help them feel better. And that felt like something bigger than me that had a hold on my heart, making it bigger. Like it was – oh man. I don't have words – stretching my little girl heart. God using **me** – and it felt good. Like an honor, a huge responsibility.*

A soft knock on her door. "Can I come in?" Tracey stuck her head around the door.

"If it's good news or a lovely chocolate snack, you can. What brings you, good-lookin'?" sliding her journal under the covers.

Tracey sat on the other bed frowning, looking at her nails. "I hate to bother you with this but I'm getting a wall from your insurance people. They are changing their story – 'we-have-new-information' crap. One week, they're saying. Aghh your wretched insurance companies – I thought Britain's system was hard. They do this horsehockey all the time.

I've pulled every trick in my considerable arsenal including a sharp note from Dr. Gomez. They won't budge." She banged the insurance papers on her thighs. "Ummh!" She tucked her shirt in. "So. You need to see Dr. Gomez – she wants you there at twelve. She's skipping lunch for this. And she's ma-ad."

"You're the best, Trace. Thanks for fighting for me. I'll be there. This sucks." Jillian leaned forward to reach for her toes and held the stretch, head dropping toward thighs. "Man, Trace. I'm just getting warmed up here. I have just begun to face into my dark night . . ."

"I know, and you're doing so well from what I hear. I wonder how the blimey insurance creeps sleep at night. I'm so sorry, sweetie." She gave Jillian's arm a squeeze and left.

And now this, she wrote. *What ever is this about? I'm scared now. No. Truly screwed now.*

~ ~ ~

Dr. Gomez welcomed her with a kind hug and a frown of frustration. "I'm so sorry, Jillian. I thought this was all set up for you when we invited you here. Coyotes! They like to play the Devil with our money." Dr. Gomez' face was flushed, her black eyes popping. Jillian heard the Spanish cadence in her angry words.

Jillian sat down across from her and crossed her arms, her lower lip trembling. "I feel so ready to do this work here now." She snagged her lips between thumb and forefinger and closed her eyes.

"You don't have to hold your feelings in, dear." Dr. Gomez reached a hand to touch her knee, just enough permission to let Jillian release. "Yes, let it out. Good healing tears."

"I don't know why – I'm confused." Jillian sputtered. "I mean, I thought this was my chance . . ."

After several moments Dr. Gomez suggested, "Maybe there's a way you can amp up your pace, Jillian. I think you can do it. I will keep pace with you but not push. Well, maybe un poquito - " She held up thumb and forefinger with a mischievous smile.

Jillian rubbed her temples in little circles for several moments. Inwardly she took the bounce. "If you think I can – I owe it to Jordan and all my relations," calling on a favorite Native American mantra. "I'll give it what I've got," lifting her chin. "What else is there to do? I can't let those insurance bastards win."

~ ~ ~

Later she walked slowly to the pond, her pace matching her deep thoughts, shoes crunching a syncopation. She tried focusing on where muscle and bone responded to brain as she walked mindfully – the impulse to step, the contact with earth, and the wonder as mind and body and earth connected.

"Hi there. I hoped those footfalls might mysteriously morph into you." Josie sat on the bench watching her approach, chuckling, belly bouncing.

Jillian's hand flew to her heart "Wo. Scared me into next week!" shaking the hand. "I'm so glad it's you, Josie. I was far out there in la-la land."

"Don't I *know* it. So what's on your mind, girl? Pull up a bench." She slid over.

"Actually? Pretty sucky day. My insurance company in its wisdom shortened my time by a week. Gotta leave Friday so I need to figure out how to cram two weeks into one. How is *that* possible?"

Josie rested palm on cheek, elbow in other hand. "Augh. Do you believe this shit? I got the same news today. I thought it was because I didn't give them sufficient cause – wasn't crazy enough for 'em. Little do *they* know. But you now – talk to me, girl."

Jillian let herself slump against Josie's high shoulder for a short respite. "I'm – naked. I'm real vulnerable. I just let this huge chasm open and now I'm afraid I won't have the time to sort it all out. Which feels a whole lot scarier than before I knew about the bloody chasm. Now I'll have to go back home to the can of worms – no, rattlesnakes – without any answers. Sorry, I don't need to dump . . ."

49

"I hear you, girl. I'm just wondering, kind of for both of us. . . " She lifted her eyes to watch a pair of hawks circling a thousand feet above. "What if this is all unfolding as it should – God having His way with us – including having each other here to spur us into the depths of ourselves where there's some deeper strength we haven't yet learned? So we have to work with what we're given? 'Cause you spark me, Jillian. I'll try to strike a few chords in you if you'll have me."

"You kiddin' me, woman? I'm in. Let's roll this party out."

They high-fived, laughing and whooping and carrying on, co-conspirators in finding the gold in the midst of all this caca.

Chapter 9

Meanwhile, back at home

Jillian saw Jordan's number come up on her phone. *Ooh!* She wanted to jump right into it. "***Hey-y-y*** sweets. God it's good to hear your voice. I miss you *so* bad. How *be* you, man?" Jillian felt familiar home joy at the sleepy sound of him.

"Hey beautiful," came his rusty voice. "Are they treating you right? You best *get* that luscious body back in this bed soon." He stretched long and luxuriously. "MM-mmm."

"OH-h yeah. So. Things all right with you, baby?" *You talk, my love. I gotta learn to listen to you better. I see now how it shifts the energy in me when Dr. Gomez listens well to me, and Dr. Jake – makes a kind of – of – space in me, an opening somehow. For something bigger than me . . .*

Long pause."Yeah. Pretty quiet here actually. Your grandpa's holding on still, likely his ornery way of pissin' everybody off. Callie told me Lacey is cool, between boyfriends, maybe a bit of a breather for her and Marco? And the boys and their rigs seemed steady yesterday – that's one day, mind you. Rad and I looked at a truck to replace that western slope rig, pretty decent, we'll see if they take our bid. Oh and the bank is not bangin' on the door yet this mornin' tryin' to turn my pockets inside out. So. How about you, my sweet honey-in-the-rock?"

"Well. I'm digging in, babe. Slow but sure. And those insurance bandits are actually helping me, I see it now, by cutting my time in half. So every day – no, hour, minute, is precious time, gets me in the now, which is a sweeter place to hang out than I ever knew. Funny sort of twist, hunh? And I've got all this good stuff I told you about - cool Norrie and Dr. Gomez and Josie for a new friend. So yeah, Jordo. I could stay here and dive deep for a decade. But I would die of missing you somewhere in the night. How's my Sky-baby doing?"

"Feisty little bugger. He looks at me like, '*You* again. So where's Mama, fool, you stableboy?' They shared a chuckle. "Doc's keepin' a close eye on the leg, says it's lookin' as good as he wants. He sure loves that horse. Maybe that's half of how he heals them."

"Ahh, my wise love. So good to just be *with* you. So simple. So the plan for Friday – I'll likely leave after lunch, about five hours' drive, after my closure meeting with my shrink."

"I'll rustle somethin' together for dinner. Love you to Jupiter and back. And Jillie? Just *be* there and don't be worrying about home. We're somehow survivin' without your long black whip."

"I hear you baby. That whip's hidden in – never mind. Love you more and I can't wait to hold you. 'Bye baby."

~ ~ ~

Jillian went to group that night ready to focus on her response to Bill Driver's death. "So. Last time I shared with you what made me a fixer – my baby brother's untimely death, and a sense of powerlessness like a five-year-old would experience in a time like that. I get that now that you helped me get it out in the open. That somehow took the blame-sting out, knowing that was normal and not freakish for a five-year-old." She looked around at the group with a diffident smile of gratitude. "And I have to leave Friday at noon now because my insurance – buzzards! So tonight I want to waste no time zeroing in on what got me here, okay?"

Max shook his head. "You and Josie getting short-sheeted by

insurance. So guys, we tighten up now. Work for one and you're working for all. Focus, troops."

Norrie jumped in. "Talk to us, Jillian. We're with," pumping her fist.

"So. I worked with a client named Bill for maybe twenty sessions six months ago. We did insightful work on an embezzlement he suffered by his cousin whom he'd brought into his business. I thought he'd thoroughly processed it, and we both agreed our work was complete for that time." She rubbed her palms on her jeans. Max's sharp radar saw something was hitting her.

"It didn't feel right to go snooping into his financial affairs after he was gone, but something wasn't sitting well, and I just now put the pieces together. It came to me in a dream that he'd been gambling recently to make up his losses. He must have taken a hit that day. I ran into him recently with his wife, all normal and chatty, and that very night I heard about his suicide. God it still gets me right here in the breadbasket." She fisted her belly as her face clouded over. "I really cared – I mean, nothing weird, just like he and I hit it hard together in the office, the kind of work that makes us all love what we do, the quality stuff." She looked at Norrie, who nodded collegially and stuck a thumb in the air.

"That's what makes being here with you folks so worthwhile for me – we all understand the great stuff about our work. It seems like truly sacred work to me. I mean, not to be high-falutin' and hinkty as Miss Josie would say . . . " She looked around at the attentive faces. "But that dream just the other night about the gambling – that's when the pieces fell into place. It wasn't my fault for missing it six months ago – it wasn't happening then."

"Righto, Jillian. So how does it feel now? In here -" Al put his hand on his belly, speaking in that way low bass of his. *How can a voice go that low?* she thought.

"It helps to share it with you all, Al, but if his widow takes me to court for criminal liability, I will be in very heavy doodoo. That's what got me here – my fear was eating me up inside. She threatened me and she seems hell-bent to make somebody pay."

Long silence. Jillian's heart pounded. Max called for a break.

Max moved to sit beside her as the group drifted out. "How's chances she'll bring suit?" he asked quietly.

"Pretty good, Max. She needs blood. She's talking to a malpractice lawyer in New York. Seems only a matter of time until she finds one willing to take this on."

"I can't see how any expert witness would testify that six months' hiatus offers any claim. But – stranger things land on court dockets. You're wise to be on alert and legally covered yourself. But not in fear. There's a major difference there, right?" Max stroked his mustache.

"I'm still in panic mostly, at least until that dream seemed to unravel it. But I hear you and I'm trying to get there. This is all new stuff for me. I just took out liability insurance a year ago because insurance requires it for third party payments. I was always told if I did honest work and didn't make promises I couldn't keep, I wouldn't need it."

"Insurance bites!" he exploded. "They're taking a bigger slice of our paychecks daily, the sleazeballs. Don't let Dr. Gomez hear me say that," rubbing the corners of his mouth. "She'll be on her soapbox right alongside me. So, Jillian, you got a choice facing you, a significant one. Let the bastards strike fear in your heart and play ball with them, or take the high road and believe in yourself and in your Higher Power's guidance."

Jillian turned to face him full on. Softly she acknowledged, "Max. That's just what I intend to do. And *damn* but it helps to hear you say it. Like it's not la-la-land thinking."

When the group resumed, she was able to track their issues as easily as old times, aware she was enjoying the process, her old confidence back.

As they disbanded, Josie came alongside her in the hall. "I'm in, my friend."

"I feel you. Thank you." Jillian was grateful when she slept like a baby that night. "Even slept through your buzz saw last night, Chicago," she told Norrie.

Chapter 10

Pits

Thursday morning. Jillian woke in a dark mood. Norrie was snoring up a symphony. *A shower – that'll reset my snakepit of a mind.* She slid in to the welcoming warmth, wondering what she'd got hold of during sleep. *Tricky dogs, these thoughts. They can take me down a rabbit hole quicker'n shit,* she pondered as she luxuriated in the bubbly cleanse.

She had learned the best way to cope with these dark thoughts was to sit down and call them in, like she'd been taught to breathe into a sore spot in the body. Just the simple awareness the breath provided usually relieved the pain. She ratcheted up the heat a notch, and as the searing water lightly pelted her skin, she imagined it penetrating through hide to heart in search of the source of this angst. *Water outside blending with the water inside the cells. Why not if we're ninety-something percent water?* she reasoned. She let the steaming water pry at her thoughts to find what it would.

Sky came to mind. *Sky? What about my big four-legged wonderboy?*

Stalwart, came the word into her mind. *Okay, what does that mean?* She cut the shower and toweled herself off to go find the word on her phone dictionary. "Strong and loyal," it read. *He surely is both of those.*

So – is he my guide to growing those qualities in me, perhaps? Am I reading this right?

She paused. No more words came. *Okay, that feels true. So I'll let you keep teaching me what you came to teach, big guy, because you haven't ever ONCE let me hang. You are the Sultan of Stalwart.* She sat on the toilet in towels, grinning like a chimpanzee, feeling loony. She laughed out loud.

Okay. If the Sultan of Stalwart is my role model in the paddock, how can I falter? Get that butt in gear, girlfriend. You know what to do. She flipped through the pictures of him on her phone, longing for him. *Won't be so hard being kicked out of here with you waiting at home, big.* She kneaded her thighs. How flabby they'd grown since Sky injured himself. *Yuck. Blobbo.*

Norrie knocked on the door. "Hey, looneytunes. Can I use the john? Gonna get messy out here soon."

"NO! Not that again," and she bolted out chortling to Norrie, cozying up with her journal for a while. *How cool these stark white pages invite me down into my core to find the words for these new thoughts,* she wrote. *Journaling makes me pry my guts open to where the words are, imperfect perhaps but at least a first stab at it. Guess I am a thoroughgoing introvert and always have been. I thought I was just shy. This feels deeper, somehow more true. Because it's not wrong, bad me, it just is how I'm geared.*

She looked out the window to the woods. A deer grazed at the edge. *Aww, and over there – her fawn with its rows of white polka dots. Taller than our Colorado mule deer.* She watched until they grazed their way into the woods. She knew then what she had to do.

Norrie returned to her bed clad in towels. "Norrie, um, can I ask you something?"

"Shoot. No, wait I can't think without caffeine. Cream no sugar, right?" She pointed two fingers toward her eyes and then at Jillian's, threw on a robe and left for the dining hall.

Jillian reread her last journal entry. *So why do I feel drawn to this deep solitude? Is it just for navel-gazing? What am I looking for way down inside me?* She willed herself to breathe and listen for an answer.

It began like a whisper when the answer came. *Deep calls to deep.*

She felt a vertigo-like flash, a light-headed spin, just for a second. It reminded her of an acupuncture treatment when the needle entered and whooshed that quick energy, followed by a calm settling in like a refreshing breeze.

I don't know what exactly this is, but it feels true. Like I'm turning inward to a place I've not known. Like finding Home. True north.

Norrie appeared with coffees and Danish. "So now. What's this revelation that's churning like a worm in your trim little belly?"

"Thanks, Norrie, good coffee. I like how nice you are. You ever hear, um, words that seem to be written on your mind?" *Oh mannn. Why am I talking about this? She'll think I'm going off, a Jesus freak or some such weirdo.*

Norrie sipped and stared. "Hm-m. Goin' deep at the first light of dawn oh GOD. Good. I like it deep and intense." She raised her eyebrows and let out a guttural chuckle. Jillian caught her meaning and snorted coffee out her nose and they lost it, cackling like brood hens.

Norrie wound down with a thoughtful look, toweling her hair. "Yeah, actually. God tells me His thoughts a lot, but for me it's more like pictures. I see whole plays, little short scenes sometimes, or paintings, and then I know what to say or do. Happens a lot when I'm working with clients. Like one friend of mine who has these amazing vivid dreams. They are so complex and full-blown and just right for her. I don't get those so much as these pictures, like I said, or photos in color and lots of detail so I can't miss the point. And then when I'm awake, I can't recall nothin' but the *feel* of it. Frustrates me bad, but that don't help much, my complainin'."

She snort-laughed again, eyes wide at Jillian, then leaned forward, forearms on thighs. "Jillie. Do you think God comes to each of us in the way we can see best? A little different for each one of His kids? And if that's so, how loving is *that*? Like He shapeshifts Hisself into a form we each get so we *notice*. That's *amazin'*." She dipped her Danish in the coffee and yummied.

"I never get to talk about this stuff, Jillie. I'm glad we got thrown together on this bus, babycakes." She affirmed her words with a lift of her Danish. "Cheers, dearie. And to You, Big Daddy, for Your slick room arrangin'." She closed her eyes, then began a riff of Amazing Grace that chilled Jillian to her bones. She came in with harmony softly, then more boldly, and they exploded into a duet of heart and voice that left them breathless, laughing.

"Wow what a voice," Jillian raved. "You sing professionally?"

"Used to, in a band in my druggin' days. That's what hauled me into the drug mess. Now it's the shower or the car." She laughed low. "Nobody asks me much now so I jus' entertain m'self whenever I feel a song comin' on me. I figure God give me this voice so He must wanta hear it once in a while."

"Norrie. Could we stay in touch when they ship me outa here? I – uh – want. . ."

"You ain't shakin' loose of me that easy, missy. Let's do it." They floated up to standing in a long embrace that felt to Jillian like an embrace of her very soul.

"There. Done deal, " Norrie affirmed with a bob of her chin. "Sistahs."

~ ~ ~

Last group for Jillian and Josie. Max asked Josie first out of respect for her seniority, and then Jillian. "Here are your questions: did you get what you came for? And did we and you do good work? You start if you will, Miss Josie. And spare us any whitewash."

Josie looked slowly around the group as if stamping each face on her memory. "I believe we did, and I did. It would be particular hell to waste a chance as rare as this for learning about ourselves. You guys asked me good questions and you did mostly honest work yourselves. So thank you each and all. I wish you were coming home with me. Except you eat too damn much." *Always end on a quip, that's Josie. Leave 'em wanting more,* Jillian smiled. A couple of people chimed in with appreciations for Josie.

"You've contributed a lot, Miss Josie. You kept us thinking and laughing. Both important here. I'm sad to see your back, woman. And you, Miss Jillian?" came Max's soft inquiry. "High points, low points? Takeaways?"

"Pretty much straight good, except I could stay here for a very long time and keep shedding layers of crazy, feels like. I'm excited to go home to my husband and my horse, and it's just as well it's in that order. I think you all helped me rip away a scab or two and dig in for treasure I didn't know was in me. I'm grateful, and I know there's more to go, guys. Real thanks to you all." She half-smiled a quirky shy grin. They liked her, her raw naked self. She could feel it – worth the sweat.

~ ~ ~

Jillian felt the true regret born of respect as she parted with Dr. Gomez. Shyly she murmured, "You mirrored a depth in me from your own guts, Dr. Gomez, so I could get a glimpse of what a wiser me looks like. And you handled the shortened time wonderfully – got right to it and shone a light around it. You truly rock. I'll be musing on you as I'm working with clients. Thank you so much," and they hugged.

"Giving is receiving, you know," Dr. Gomez said, holding Jillian's hands with gusto. "I learned from your courage and good intent. Go with God in grace. And – you got enough, I know that. You'll use it well. Your clients are lucky to have found you."

"Well. Okay then," and Jillian shone a smile. As she drove toward home, she felt some new spark, a peaceful and solid place inside.

Maybe those insurance squirrels did me a favor after all. I think I'm ready for home and my two studs.

Chapter 11

Re-entry

Jillian drove the long roads home in a changing inner landscape that mimicked the interesting exterior one – mountains spilling over plains, pasturing cattle, a lone antelope running swiftly down a hillside, and a singular red-tailed hawk soaring on currents for pure joy.

Show-off! Just because you can, you lovely, she sent out to him. *I can't know if you're a messenger from my good man Bill Driver, little bird-friend, but may I claim you as a sentinel from beyond anyway? The Buddhists talk about Don't Know Mind – is that the same thing as Mystery? The transcendent? My heart knows so much more than my mind, I see that now. When I get out here on this wild open road, my thoughts take flying leaps and I feel connected to all that is, and I know that this energy is real and is somehow carrying me along, and that it is truly this simple. Life is. Isness. Just carrying me along in it like you soar on it, bird-friend.*

As she drove she felt the warm glow of anticipation spread from mind to heart and out into legs and arms. She remembered the Yoga teacher at the clinic, a pert soul named Jennifer, who showed them how to send energy through their chakras, the whirling energy centers. Jillian had sensed an important tool in these seven centers and had begun playing with them by simply breathing into each one. She thought of it now so she wiggled her butt deeper in her seat and took her mind to a few inches below her crotch, called kundalini or root chakra, and up through the center of her body through each chakra slowly, mindfully, to just above her crown, the seventh chakra. When she reached the crown chakra, she sent her breath out into the cosmos. *Ooh that feels lighter – hm-mm.*

It's amazing this new sense of being in my own body, of Spirit as energy, that which can't be seen in form like some bearded guy in the sky, but everywhere as spirit or energy moving. She practiced flowing the energy again from crotch to crown very slowly, pausing in each chakra until it felt full, satiated, and she smiled slightly as she drove along in this mystery.

She felt a fresh aliveness, a tingling in her belly and forehead. The wonder of sharing this with Jordan and Sky and Callie made her heart sing. Then – *how in heck do you do this work on a horse? Where are his chakras anyway, and must I stand on a ladder to reach them?* And she burst out laughing. *I'll google it,* she decided. *Thank you, Stanford techies. You have made endless information so accessible for us.*

Now a big new question popped into her mind. *So, If everything has energy or spirit livening it, then is everything simply energy? Moving molecules, not solid as we're taught? E=MC2. Whoa. M is mass. Let's see – I remember that means there's a lot of energy in any mass, even tiny things. And if our bodies have energy moving as freely as Jennifer showed us with her pendulum, we are power-packed. DA-amn. She let her mind wander though that opening as she moved through the open Colorado highway.*

Finally. She pulled into the yard to find her man leaning against the porch post, grinning and smoking.

"Well hello there, cowboy," she crooned. "Busy tonight?"

He shouldered off the post to amble over with his long saddle-bowed legs. She climbed out of the car and enfolded him with a pure pleasure cry. "That's what's so sexy about you," as she squeezed him. "Never in a hurry. You're a . . . a slow invitation all the way in." She leaned back in his arms to have an eyeful.

He nibbled her neck. "You taste like forbidden fruit." He squeezed her hard. "We never been apart this long, right? Since what, ninth grade?"

"That's about how I remember it. How lucky are we? Can we walk out to see the boy?"

Jordan took her hand and walked with her to the paddock. Sky saw them and walked up to the gate, snorting. Jillian hustled through the fence to reach both arms around his neck and hold on. "Oh-h buddy. Oh **man** I've missed you guys bad. Mm-m-mm."

Jordan fetched a scoop of oat mash for Sky, who gobbled it out of Jillian's hands. The tickling of his quivering lips and warm breath felt primal. "Damn, boy. It's so-o *good* to feel you and smell you."

The sun crested over the red rocks as they all stood in close. The temperature began its drop perceptibly. Bright blue sky started deepening into dusk.

"It's so awful good to be home," Jillian whispered. "Let's go on in, cowboy."

~ ~ ~

Next day Jillian was in her office with a woman named Jenn whose sixteen-year-old daughter was experimenting with marijuana and "probably a bunch of other things that would horrify me that I don't even want to know about. But then again I *do* want to know . . . I'm pretty sure she's sexually active by the hints she throws. Like, 'Oh, I'm not into Jack anymore, Mom, he's seriously dorky'."

"Translate: not fast enough for you?" Jenn told Jillian. "I mean I don't *say* that to her but . . ."

"Then it's 'I'm into Zach for a *while* now, Mom. He's so . . . he has these long eyelashes and eyes that . . . whatever. I can't explain it to you – he's just so . . .' The glassy eyes go dreamy here, voice trails off. Then, 'you wouldn't understand, Mom. It's different now. Times have changed from your teenage, Mumsy, it's too much to explain, I gotta *go*.' A breezy peck on the cheek and she's gone." Jenn looked off into space. "She's spiking moody like a yo-yo, flying high one minute and slamming doors the next. She treats her little brother like a brainless hunchback with bad teeth. Except when those glassy eyes with the huge pupils focus on something she wants, like his help with her trigonometry. Then she's seductively sweet and the poor boy melts into her spell like a hungry hypnotized zombie."

Jenn sipped her water. "It's like she's trying to keep one foot in her relationship with me and her brother and her dad, and walk the teen world like a serious player, back and forth, back and forth. Watch a tennis match lately?" and she grinned with raised eyebrows, inviting Jillian's feedback.

Jillian nodded, making her eyes reflect empathy. "Anything like when you were sixteen and navigating whole new worlds without a compass?"

"Sort of. Yeah. But I *knew* my mom was clueless. She was so into herself, *her* work, *her* friends. I *try* to keep up because my mom didn't even try and I know how shitty alone that feels." Jenn shook her curly head. "So, I go to all her lacrosse games, all her basketball games, keep up online with her schoolwork, with *both* kids' stuff. But this *is* a different world now and – oh. **O-ohh**. I just got something. This is about staying open to *her* world, what *she's* feeling and thinking, right? Like stepping back and letting her take the lead? Wow, that was a whammy insight. But not hover like some of these moms who micromanage their poor kids. Whoa – I got my work cut out here, Jillian, *thank* you. That's a fine new line to walk. Like when to hold 'em and when to fold 'em." She picked up her things and left with a see-you-next-week over her shoulder, her head shaking in wonder like someone who just learned the sky was falling.

Jillian gave a small smile, lower lip pursed, at the woman's disappearing back. "Go. Kick some butt. Even if it's yours. Can't wait to hear how it plays out." Jillian got up to fix herself a cup of tea, musing on the power of the connection that held her keen awareness of Jenn the whole hour.

"Damn. This shit works."

Chapter 12

Reality sandwich

Jordan reached over to pull Jillian in close, hungrily inhaling the familiar lavender scent she wore. "God we are *so* good together. You are so yummy – you even smell yummy – and you were so absent from this haven of ours." Jordan had no difficulty willing himself to put any tough stuff aside when her beautiful responsive body was this near, and eager for his.

But Jillian was spilling with talk, wanting to share all about the trip and the changes she was experiencing as the scales fell away from her eyes. So much new on her heart . . . especially for her man.

"Woman. Did that lawyer father of yours never teach you first things first?" his hand sliding the length of her silky thigh, kneading imploringly.

Afterward he propped himself up on pillows to have a proper smoke. His satisfied smile was twin to hers. "Now you can talk. All of it."

She gently probed his pecs with the heel of her hand. "Mm-m. Why? Why can't we just bask in lusciousness? For a week? That yummy goodness sure put all the other doodoo in perspective as you knew it would. You're always way ahead of me, and you can't expect me to *like* that. Hard on the ego, y' know?"

He smiled in that sardonic way and blew his inhale at the ceiling.

After a while she kissed his neck and said, "Okay *now, damn ya'*. The best way to share it all is in this - " and she fished her journal out of her bag, holding it out. My soul-talk place. "Okay here's one – um, maybe it's a little, I dunno – okay here goes nothin': *"I feel these pages inviting me to drop down in to find the words for my thoughts. Journaling softens me to ready my heart for opening. A bona fide introvert – guess I've always been. Do I mind that or is it okay with me?"* He responded with a dorky look. She shook her head, pursed her lips.

She tried another page. "Okay then how about this? *You find your true self in the mystery. Deep calls to deep.* That was something bigger than me talking, an energy, a spirit, God maybe? Mind-boggling, hunh?"

Jordan basked in relaxation, eyes closed. "Sounds like you got your insurance money's worth in Kansas. You put your whole self in like you do, you gutsy crazy broad. Don't know if I could. And – energy is spirit is God as you see it? I dunno, Jillie. I'll hafta ponder this." He took a last drag on his smoke, tamped it out and turned toward her.

"Look. I didn't want to dump this on you while you were at the dude ranch, but . . . you ready for some hard facts, babe? My turn?"

She nodded. "Yeah. And – dude ranch – that works. So talk, man. Your turn. All of it. I really want to know."

"Okay. Lay of the land as we know it this day. Radford's still with us, and Sark. Lefty and Monty hadda walk when money got too tight. I'm not sure we're gonna hold on here. It's obvious the bank is nervous. I'm – I feel like such a shit-ass loser. Dad and then Mom held this all together for all those years and paid for our college and now I can't even – Jesus." His tone had sunk to that raspy scared sound. He crossed his arms and glowered.

"Baby – please don't do this to yourself. Do you realize how downright unreal it sounds? This is change, is all. We just have to rein in a little and figure out -"

"Jillian. Hear me, love. I'm up to my ass in bills. We owe a lotta money for equipment I don't have and no prospects of getting it. I don't know how Rad and Sark are hanging on. Living off their women, likely.

Shit. Some boss man." His voice was gravel, his throat constricted. "You hearing me girl?"

Hearing your shame and self-blame shouting – no, screaming. I sure am. "Jord. I *do* know. I've been watching your shoulders sink, your frown deepen, and your smoking increase every single day for years. This is paradigm shift time, and I don't know what's coming but – the signs are pointing to some kind of real change for us. Not catastrophe, shift. I can see yours because I see that I gotta figure out how to do my own. Scary as hell but somehow *right,* you know?"

He jerked out of bed and strode stiff-legged to the shower, shaking his head.

Jillian curled up in a ball. ***So** down on himself. He'd never be that hard on anyone else but he's merciless to his own aces self so – help, Whoever. Please,* she begged. *It's frickin' past time and I'm just waking up. Thank God I finally am. Too late to help that dearest man?*

~ ~ ~

Next night the phone rang at about eight-thirty. Jordan fished out his cell phone. "Yeah Rad. How's it with you, man?" in his upbeat tone that fooled no one, massaging the back of his neck with his strong fingers. Long listen. "Where'd you get ahold of that?" in an unbelieving tone.

Jillian reread the same line in her book four times. *His voice sounds hopeful. Good news?*

"Wo. I don't believe – yeah, gimme the contact info and I'll think about it, talk with Jillie – he wrote it on an envelope. "Got it man. Don't know what I'd do without – yeah, and thanks my man." He hung up and sank on the couch, staring into nowhere, his hands opening and closing on his thighs.

"Well?" She stuck a finger in her book. "Talk to me about -"

"That guy is – I wouldn't be – okay so he heard one of the assistant coaches at CU got fired for a dirty urine and they're looking for a ready fill-in. Part time. I could negotiate salary 'cuz they're up the creek – whaddya think?" turning to her as if just remembering she was there.

"I say make the call now. Coach at prestigious Colorado University? Your shoulders just lifted two notches. Energy at work -"

He lit a smoke, checked his watch. "Nobody there now. First thing in the morning. Man! Back on the courts to save the farm? Decent money for pure *play*?" He jumped up and went to the kitchen for wine and their good glasses.

Jillian winked at the ceiling. *Thanks. You're quick. And accurate – I see you don't play around. I might learn to trust you if you keep this up, whoever you are.*

He called CU first thing in the morning and left a message. The athletic director called back mid-morning. "Thanks for your call, Mr Nicholson. I've heard that you were pretty hot in your day. You were on my list but I already lined somebody up. Damn. I'll keep your contact info and if anything opens, you'll have first crack, I promise you that. Let's get the paperwork rolling meanwhile, OK?"

Jordan thanked him and hung up.

Jillian tied her sneakers on and looked up seriously. "Yeah, I heard, but something's shifting. That's a step, right? Let's keep looking for options and doing whatever legwork we can. Who knows if that guy will work out? This is all mostly hearsay so far."

He held his disappointment until she left, then kicked the truck tire with all his might. "Ow-w! Shit." *Maybe I'll check out my hoop skills just in case.* He went to the gym for a pick-up game that afternoon. "Not entirely hopeless," he told Jillian at dinner with the hint of a smile.

Chapter 13

Whose circus, whose monkeys?

Jillian was in her office pondering the latest in the thickening file of Lisa Driver threats. This one was an email stating that she was talking with a New York attorney who specialized in cases of "unprofessional and unethical conduct." The more of these "ankle biters" showed up, the more unhinged and desperate Lisa was becoming, or so it appeared.

She read it over several times, then between the lines as she nibbled on a cracker. She dropped it in an email file as Dr. Jake advised. "Just a quick read to see if they require any action, then file and forget. I'd look to my own emotional progress through this process, Jillian," he had advised. "She's just saber-rattling so far. In my experience threats like these often drift away out of boredom. You'll know if and when action is called for, and I'll be your back-up guy."

Easy for him to say, thought Jillian. *He's not the one losing the sleep. Wonder if he's ever faced something remotely like this.*

But she needed his clarity in this turbid water. *Companioning in the dark places,* she thought. *It helps me get on the other side of the equation and know what it's like for clients as I witness with them through their stuff. Like Dr. Gomez and Dr. Jake are witnesses for me.* She took a long breath, then chuckled at a new image in her mind. *Now when I catch myself drifting toward fear, I picture a bunch of long-armed monkeys swinging and screeching through the jungle, like Norrie does. Takes the sting out. And if I'm alone, I scratch my armpit and "whough-whough," a little. I mean, it beats that cortisol rush of fear creeping up my belly. So Lisa, you're actually giving me the gift of new choice.*

She heard from Norrie once about a new group she was singing with and how invigorating it was to be singing again. She fired back a newsy reply but heard no more. Josie was on it though, emailing and the occasional call which kept their connection growing.

She rang Josie one hot afternoon. "Hey my trusted buddy. How're your moods? You holding steady down there in your sublime desert landscape?" *I simply love this cool fun soul and that feels good. Real.*

"I've still got a grip, yeah, thanks to God, wherever She might be having lunch today. St. John's wort seems to be helping. It's subtle, and I still cry some but the tears feel like release instead of depression. Family's holding, all that testosterone sustainin' 'em, I suppose, kinda pickles 'em I guess. How about you? Did the ceiling fall in when you got home?"

"You know, it was great to get home, lucky-duck-me. Jord's business is dragging, but there's a new something in the wind. I had a lot of hours driving home to put together the pieces I got from you all. And that chakra stuff Jennifer taught us? I use that now in 'reading' clients – their energy, their body language. I'm quicker on the uptake now because I can feel their stuck energy and understand what that's telling me. It's fascinating! Different for each person. Keeps me more alert and less, um, clinical, in my head. I've balanced a few experimentally inclined folks' chakras who are willing to let me. One woman, Beth? She said she never felt so good after a counseling session and the effect lasted for days. Said she felt like she'd had a massage. Whoee."

"You're onto something, ain't you? Good on ya'. You're fun, kid. Daring to dwell at the edge."

Jillian stretched her free hand out wide and observed it. *I love this. The sweet taste of connection.* "You inspire *me*, Jos, with your kick-butt courage and sharp mind and that rapier wit. You *got* to keep it coming."

"Yeah, well, I will if you will. I can do that much for a pal, though you're younger and far cuter than I ever tried to be."

Jillian hung up. *I wonder – does she have any idea of the brightness in and around her? Am I getting off-the-rails weird here? Does anybody else think about this stuff? Maybe Tory – I'll take a run with her and check this out.*

Tory met her for lunch and a trail run the next day. "You know anything about chakras, Tor?"

"A little. Sanscrit word meaning whirling energy, right? The seven energy centers that our auras send out from our bodies?"

Jillian stared at her beloved friend. "Damn, girl. You don't miss much. Am I likely to get run out of town on a rail for working with clients this way if the word gets out? Which it always does. How about 'witch' for a label?"

"Yeah, you might, anywhere but Boulder or Berkeley." She yanked on Jillian's floppy sun hat and started singing. "Oh – oh – witchy woman. . ." and boogeying wild moves.

Jillian cracked up. "Always two steps ahead of me. Like Jordan. I hate that."

Chapter 14

Jordan

It was July 15th. Jordan watched his dad's old truck come up the lane from the kitchen window mid-morning. Lucia was driving slowly to avoid stirring up dust clouds that had gritted her porch so peskily when she lived here, which she did not miss. This had been a dry summer. Fire hung in the tinder, the dead grasses.

Scott rode shotgun, scowling and wiping his brow. The trouble in his eyes showed Jordan that something was up.

Jordan knew every line and mood etched on those aging faces. He grimaced, threw on his hat and went out to greet them, hugging first his mom, then around the back of the truck to pull the wheelchair out for his dad. "Hey rowdies. What're you doin' to my topsoil, peelin' in here on two wheels? You better come on in here then." From the pasture Sky whinnied hello to his buddy Scott.

Scott heard and grinned his half-smile to Jordan. His face muscles had never come back fully since the stroke. He leaned in to meet his son's forehead with his and lingered there until Jordan stepped back. "Row-dies," Scott slurred, grinning at his son.

Lucia looked up at her two rangy men from her scant five feet, a grin on her full lips. "Oh mi quieros – where would I be without you two – mi triste vaqueros." She dug in her purse for a hankie.

Scott dropped into his wheelchair as Jordan steadied it, guiding him with a sure hand on his shoulder. "Miserable cowboys, she calls us, Pop."

Scott's forefinger pointed from his eye to Scott's and they chuckled.

The deck held its inviting shade from the big cottonwood. They moved up to it gratefully.

Lucia blubbered mostly in English her version of Missy's crisis last night, which was was brought them out. Family business that needed sharing.

"She was mugged outside her apartment building. Oh God . . ." She closed her eyes and sat shaking her head, squeaky moans mewing out of her throat, her hankie dabbing at the wet.

Scott squinted up at the red rocks, his wide leathery hand on her knee. Jordan noted his other hand dangling in his lap, opening and closing slightly. "Sumbitch. If I could f-f-fly. . ." He spat.

He's making a fist, Jordan saw. "She okay, Mom?" *I'll fly out there and take the bastard out for you, Dad.* He rubbed an eyebrow hard, breathing deep, grinding his teeth. He scraped his boots under him and stood. "Lemme get you guys some iced tea," and he stalked off.

They nodded. Jordan's way when he was mad – having a think, cooling off, his folks knew. Lucia wiped her eyes, then leaned over to kiss Scott as Jordan returned.

Strong love, Jordan thought. *Now there's somethin' to admire. That still warms my gut at forty, for chrissakes.*

He put their tea down with some scones and butter. "Shit, man, I hate that she's so far away. So *is* she okay, Mom?"

"Si. She's okay. She carries that spray – what's it called? Meece? Mace. Yeah, that's it. She carries that in her hand when she has to go out at night. She says that's what saved her. She sprayed in hees face and he yell 'My eyes!' and let go. She RAN. She smart girl, right, Scott?"

"She izz," he nodded. "Get 'er a do-og. . ."

"Your dad would feel better if she got a big fierce watchdog for protection." She left the question on the table for family discussion, gesturing that it was open.

"Good idea, Dad. Can she have a dog where she lives?" Jordan turned his hat brim around to shade his eyes. *I could look around for a big dog and fly it out to New York for her.*

Lucia said, "It's sometheeng we could do. I hate her being so far away when she needs her family close to her. I'll ask her about the dog." Her hands rubbed her arthritic knees. "So, Jordo. How're theengs with you and Jeelian?" ready for his news now.

She has that Spanish way of letting her feelings flow. That why she's easy to be around? That how she ran this outfit so long, feisty little shit that she is? "We're holdin' on, Ma. It's tough." He fished in his shirt pocket for a smoke and lit it. "We're down to two trucks since a couple of weeks. Gas being sky-high and equipment worse, it's a squeeze play most of the time, **you** sure know. Radford's hanging in with us, and Sark. The others hadda move on, which helps some, cuts the overhead but also the cash flow. Rad and I are lookin' at a replacement rig for the western slope run that looks pretty decent."

I hate telling them this hard stuff because they know all the stupid grungy details, they lived this for years. Good thing we didn't tell them about Jillian's rest spa – they would have had *something to worry about. But they like shootin' the shit about the business so I gotta give them a full measure. I wonder if Mom's emotions on her sleeve bugs me because I don't much like feelin' my own, especially my failures. Dad's like me, holds it all in. That Latina nature of hers, like Missy's – but the upside is, we never once wondered if she loved us.*

"You won't get ulcers, Mama. Wish I could let it all hang out like you women. I smoke my feelings," frowning at his cigarette. He shifted in his chair. "So – Rad came up with a great idea, a part-time coaching job at the college he heard about, but it was filled already when I asked. The athletic director said he'd keep me on file. That could keep us in groceries for a while."

"Sounds just made for you, Jordie," she gushed. He watched her mist up again. It hit him then how worried she'd been about him. She muffled into her hankie, "Mi grandma used to say 'Holy tears, Lucita. Good tears." Now she was laughing at her emotional nature.

"Your fiery Meheecan spirit, Mama. You and Missy. Keeps you light, ready for anything. Like snappin' a towel at our disappearing butts."

Lucia caught her son's attempt at shifting the topic. She searched his eyes with that let's-hear-it-all stare of hers. "We had trouble making payroll every stinkin' month of the year, Jord."

"Yeah, Mom, I – look, you don't want – Missy's in trouble here . . . "

"And you're not? Come on, son. What? You losing the business? Is that it?"

Jordan took a long drag, looking from father to mother, then looked away. This was hard talk.

Scott got words out first. "Ti-imes diff-f-rent. Not yo-uur faultt. Economy ba-ad . . ."

Lucia leaned in. "We c'n help some, Jordan, tide you over. Just tell us."

"There's no freakin' way, Mama. Me'n Jillian are on it. Just – keep us in your thoughts, yeah?"

Scott nodded and covered his son's hand with his good hand. His eyes drifted closed, his lips moving.

Lucia felt a fresh tear leak. "Not a day ever passes that I don' pray for you an' Missy an' Jeelian, mi hio, an' hold you up to mi Dios. Since you were leetle bebe in my arms," and she cradled an air baby and rocked it tenderly.

"Aww, Ma, c'mon, drink your tea. Too damn hot for all this snivellin'."

Chapter 15

Dream

Jillian woke from a bad dream, lying beside snoring Jordan. While she could still remember, she picked over each character in the dream – who they might be to her, what they did, and why they were showing up in her dream.

This is wild. Those figments of my dreams are so REAL. I gotta tease this more into the open with my journal and coffee.

She slid slowly out of bed and padded downstairs with journal in hand. The clock on the kitchen wall read 4:20 a.m. She started a pot of coffee and sat in the window seat waiting for it to perk. The stars in their velvet indigo vastness looked like forever. A sliver of moon shone a surprising bright glow. *I love this magical place. I love my life and Boulder and this ranch and that humongous wide sky and You-Whoever! Ah – I like that name – that works for today.*

So now. What was that freaky dream again? Ah – Callie at the hospital to visit Grandpa, sitting beside his bed but there's nobody in the bed. Why is she sitting there? Now she's talking to an empty bed. Sad. Symbolic of his non-presence perhaps? Nobody Home Grandpa. Maybe this dream is for Cal – a dream by proxy. So I don't need to interpret, just share it?

Coffee ready. Oh yeaahh. Damn that smells fine. She walked coffee and journal into the living room and snuggled into the sofa, covering herself and stroking a heavenly soft raspberry fleece. She wrote: *I'm learning to listen to Jordan more mindfully. Hard to keep my mouth shut and not fix, but he is talking more so it's worth the teeth-clamping. He seems so down on himself these days. His folks came by to tell him Missy had been mugged – country girl in the Big Apple. He thought he should find a watchdog and take it to her but cussed himself for not having the cash or the time. I bit my tongue off.*

She paused to read what she'd written. Picking up the pen, she closed her eyes in meditation for a moment, then put pen to paper. *How about a bonus for my man, Universe? He needs a break and soon would be none too soon.* She looked at the prayer that had tumbled out. *Damn! I wouldn't have written that or even thought it before. Who is writing through me? My muse? You-Whoever? The ghost of Christmases past?* She closed her eyes and felt a warm ripple of energy from crown to belly. *Wo.* She put palms to cheeks and wondered.

In a while she heard Jordan thudding downstairs. *I must have dozed off.* She tucked the journal under the cushion and went to get him coffee. She heard him yawning on the couch. "What's up, Kookaburra? Couldn't sleep?"

She came to sit close beside him. He traced a vein on her hand, mumbling thanks and picking up his coffee. "I was done sleepin'," she said. "Had a goofy dream I was trying to figure out but I think it was for Callie and just came through me for her." She described it to Jordan. He raised his eyebrows.

"Think it might mean Clark's passed on, the empty bed?" Always the practical one. He sipped his coffee and peered at her over the brim.

"Aah. Hadn't thought of that. I was thinking about Cal. I'll check with Mom today. What've you got going on today?"

"Ordinary stuff – muck out the barn, shore up that weak spot on the corral fence before Sky gets impaled again, put in a post or two that's rotted out. Rad's truck needs some timing work. He left it for me to tinker with this weekend. Another day on the ranch, another dollar three eighty." He lit his first smoke. "Ahh-h."

"If I could do one thing to make your day a tad brighter, what might it be, my love?" gently kneading his shoulder.

"What you're doing right this minute. You've got twenty minutes to quit it." He kissed her nose.

"I have a hunch about that coaching job, don't know why. Just seems like it has your name on it." She took a swig of coffee. "You think?"

He nodded "Now that I'm oiling up these bones practicing, I kind of think so too, even though it seems nutso to say it, like I might jinx it. But you say I gotta claim it as mine, right? Believe in it and don't tell anyone?"

"So you DO listen to me once in a while. Had me fooled."

"I ain't about to give you the satisfaction, Kooka. Gotta keep you guessin' to hold your interest."

Jillian rubbed the sleepy dust from her eyes and went to the kitchen for a refill and a call to her mom. Sary had always been a dawn riser.

Sary yawned. "I was just getting around to calling you. Your grandpa is slipping away, and though it might be mean of me, I hope it's soon. It's exhausting your dad and Corbett. There, dammit, I said it. Oh, and Corbett had a biopsy on a lump in her breast." Sary sniffed. "Not good. The dear soul – she gives and gives to that selfish old coot, like Jeb does. Pisses me off." Sniff. "Sorry honey."

"Mom. Let it fly. I'm just listening, like you've done for us all these years. About time I give back some decent ear time."

"Ah, Jillie, that's really sweet. Thank you. I want to push ahead on finishing this book, up over the crest of the hill, but it has seemed too selfish when all hell is breaking loose here. So thanks for hearing me out."

"Any way I can help you launch the book? Meals? Massage? Reading your work? What?" *I like that I mean this, actually want to. That's new. Damn, feels good. I'm not a horrible selfish brat.*

Sary thought a moment. "You know, I think it's this, your listening to me with those open ears of yours. Something about that gets my thoughts flowing. And when I see it helps me find my answers - hell, questions even – I pass it on to your Dad. So it spreads itself. It's not even hard, just means zipping my lips for a few minutes."

"Well okay then. Better get rolling on our day here. Love you Mama Ducky."

"Fare thee well, my girl. Love you to Jupiter and back."

~ ~ ~

Later Callie called as Jillian stood trimming Skye's whiskers in the barn. "Hey bossy pants. You outa that sack yet?"

"Yes-I'm-outa-that-sack. Yeesh. What's on your mind this morn, sissy of mine?" She looked around at the dust motes riding sun rays, the worn old boards of the stalls, the sun filtering through spider webs. She breathed in the familiar horse and hay smells that heralded Home for her and she smiled.

Skye nickered for her attention, or perhaps the carrot in her pocket, so she appeased him with it while she checked in with Callie. "Jord and I were talking about having you guys over for dinner tonight. I had a dream I want to share with you. Any chance you're free?" Jillian stroked Skye's cheek with her knuckle. *Ah the feel of this great gentle beast. Must be illegal or obscene or at least fattening to love this much.*

"Uhm. First let me fill you in and see if you still want us, okay?" Callie's voice lowered.

"This as ominous as you sound?" Jillian felt her breathing go shallow.

"Ahh. Sucks beyond sucking. Marko told me what I already knew but didn't want to ever hear him say – he's been having an affair. Jesus but this tears me up, Jill. And for God's sake don't tell Mom. That'll be the end of him in her mind. You know how she gets about infidelity – ranks right alongside mass murder."

"I am *so* sorry, Cal. This is so – God. This hurts *me* for you. Jesus." She closed her eyes to let it burn its way down into her and get over with. *Aghhh. How* **could** *you, Marko? What the hell?* "How are *you* doing, honey?" Jillian could taste the yearning for Callie's struggles to just *stop.*

"How about Jord grills us up some of your fave steak and baked potatoes around seven? And I promise I won't start this conversation with Marko unless he – maybe we can, you know, ease through this like a normal family might." *How in hell WOULD a normal family handle this? She pondered, raising an eyebrow. This is a sea change for Cal. My part is just to listen. Oh, and not rip Marko's fucking lungs out. I trusted him with my SISter. And I love the asshole.*

"You're a good sis, Jill. I'll ask him and get back to you. Later."

Jillian thought to take coffee and cookies out to Jordan at the pasture fence and prep him for an interesting night with his brother- and sister-in-law. "Hey sweets. Guess who's coming to dinner?" as she set out a picnic blanket.

"Gimme one sec - " Bam-m – the hammer struck. "There, you prick. And stay in." The new post stood out like a fresh patch on an old shirt. He reached for his coffee and gulped. "Nice, Jillie. You'll make some dude a fine wife one day."

"Yeah right, Goober. Now park that butt here one time. We gotta talk." She leaned in to kiss him roundly.

"So what grave matter -" stroking his Sigmund Freud goatee.

"So. Mister Marko dropped a bomb. He's been having an affair with some old girlfriend in Rome. Callie knew but didn't want to hear him say it. I invited them for grilled steaks and bakes around seven, yah? A little arsenic for his salad?"

He took a cookie. "And we're not gonna bring it up unless they do," they finished in chorus. Their synchronicity made them chuckle.

"I'm off duty on Saturdays," she reminded both of them, pointing a forefinger at the air. "How about we just BE together? A weird family having another of their weird family meals on the deck. We might even dig up some laughs or some interesting current topics from the world stage, or watch a movie. Imagine!"

Chapter 16

Dinner

Sometime around seven of a fine Saturday night, Marco's Jeep pulled up in front of the Nicholsons' home. Jillian and Jordan looked at each other with questioning expressions. *Do we have this?* Jillian mouthed 'I'm off duty', hands up in surrender. Jordan held up one pointer finger as he stirred the margaritas. "Sister," he mouthed back.

Onesie tonight, she whispered, curtsying elaborately. They were both spiffed out in crisp jeans and bright shirts to signal a festive evening.

Callie and Marko came hello-ing into the kitchen with a spinach and kale salad, a tray of stuffed mushrooms and serious faces. Callie put her salad bowl on the counter, squeezed Jordan's shoulder, and melted into her sister. Then she sniffed, blew her nose on a hankie, and threw her shoulders back. Jillian fist-bumped her.

Marko put down his hors d'ouevres tray and leaned on the counter, awkwardly looking around at no one. Jordan said "Hey man" and poured their drinks, walking one over to Marko and gripping his arm briefly. Jillian moved warily toward Marko, hugged him quickly, then held him out with a warning look. "I'm having a whole lot of mixed feelings, brother. I'm just sayin'. Sister feelings. Some downright homicidal." She fanned her face with her hand and went to Jordan's side, looking up into his face.

Marko looked at the floor, cracked his knuckles. Then he was snuffling, his face in his hands. They all stood watching him. *There it is, that's the guy I thought he was, and that looks guilty as hell,* thought Jillian. *Those tears say he's still with us, that he cares. Feels like shit. He oughta, the fucker. He broke our trust. He best not be faking those tears.*

Callie fumbled with the salad cover, dropping it all on the floor. She bent to pick it up as a strangled sound came out of her.

Jordan slid his arm around Jillian and kissed her head.

Marko dropped to help Callie. "Three second rule apply at this ranch?" he asked Jordan.

"Not a second more," Jordan deadpanned solemnly.

Marko stood and looked at each face with a pinched look. "This is all my bad, I know that. Callie has been Santa Maria herself. I ran into an old girlfriend, don't even know – just happened. Stupida!" and he banged his head with his fist. "I screwed up bigtime. I owe you, my love, and you my family a major amend. And," he cleared his throat, "my promise to you all that it is done and I learned how much my family means to me. You've been so strong, Cal . . ." He sucked in his lips, looking around with an anxious frown.

They all looked to Callie who closed her eyes. They watched a host of feelings tumble across her face. Finally, "I'm going with that, Marko." She leaned on the counter, hand out in front as if claiming the space. "We've got two beautiful kids to teach how you get through shit like this. Half of me wants to rip a few of your body parts off, you son-of-a-bitch, and the other more than half loves you and always will. The only mate I've ever wanted. So that's how the hell I feel. But split up a family? Nah." She drew in a deep breath and looked to Jillian. "I know this goes without saying, but just – no one squeaks to Mom and Dad, deal?"

Jordan roused himself to hand the women their drinks. "Wisely done, Cal. I'm with you guys." He lifted his glass to them. "We'll get through this too. What the hell else would we do? Can't dance."

Jillian looked at the floor. "I respect you for this, sissy. Smart and clear and no bullshit. And you came clean and you seem to mean it, Marko, so I can love you *and* be pissed until I'm done with it. You ever hurt my sister again and we're done, mister." She glared, shook her head, and lifted her glass. "Don't *make* me call Cousin Guido." She wiped three fingers across her neck, a grin poking through.

"So now, unless anybody has more to say, that's history. How're the Broncos lining up this season, dudes? Oh, and Cal, I gotta tell you about the dream I had – I think it was for *you*," and she took Callie's arm and walked her out to the living room.

Jillian's phone rang. They listened to her say, "Ah, Mom, I'm sorry, sweetheart. How's Daddy doin'?" Pause. "Yeah, Cal and Marko are here for dinner. How about I stop over in the morning? I'll have Cal call you then. Love you, Mama. You've been a real trooper. And – I'm glad it's over. We'll pray for him. Yeah, head him upward instead of where he was hell-bent for." They shared a little co-conspirator laugh and hung up.

They looked to her, knowing. Jordan asked softly, "Clark?"

She nodded, flopping down in her chair. She looked over at Callie. "So. The old goat is daid." *Why don't I feel anything? Sad for Dad, is all. Relieved for Grandma and Mom. Not much to miss.*

Callie put her fingers through her hair. "Well. Wraps up a perfect evening, hunh?"

Marko moved over to Callie and pulled her up into his arms. "I'm so sorry, baby. *So* very sorry."

As if by some offstage signal, the four slid together, standing there, sniffles and murmurs and chuckling and clearing of throats. Callie drew her head back slowly and declared, "A shit-ass day in the Tanner family if ever there was one!" And she hooted a "Hooah!" and relief rippled through them, inciting wicked snorting laughter.

"I'll drink to that," Marko offered, and they were off again.

So this is how a weird family gets through shit. Talking it out, spitting mad, and then the laughing. Jillian chortled and went to crank up the music.

Chapter 17

Legalities

Back in the office on a Monday morning, Jillian felt drawn to look in Bill Driver's file for fine points she might glean from a now perspective. *Feels squirmy to face this but maybe it'll give me some clarity. I believe Dr. Jake would agree with this. "Look it over from every which way; consider all the possibilities, and when you're sure you're done, look for three more," he often counsels me.*

Several threads stood out as she read through the notes: "Worried he'll lose their home." And "we discussed his possible talking with Lisa about investing her money in more aggressive stocks." *Red flag. He was questioning the sanity of that, assessing the risks and his own knowledge of the system. I remember that conversation. He was fidgeting, drumming fingers on knees. I referred him to a reputable stockbroker I know for a second opinion. In the follow-up conversation I think I remember he did consult with Bernie and then felt confident in the direction he was going. But now I wonder – did that work out as he hoped?*

And notes from a month later: "Lost ground with start-up stock. Not sleeping. Drinking more." *How could I have slid over that? No notes on how I responded - and I don't remember this conversation. I need to be more precise in note-taking in case it goes to court. You're walking right into Lisa's trap there, girl. If you'd been on your toes...*

She took the notes to supervision with Dr. Jake and read them to him.

He leaned back and stared at the ceiling, laced fingers holding his head, graying hair poking out its want of a trim. Jillian felt a pang of guilt for making him work this hard, mixed with fear that he could judge her or even not want to work with her anymore, that she was too much *some*thing. She smoothed her skirt, fussed the Kleenex box into line with the table edge.

A chasm opened in her, an icy fear oozing through her veins. So much was at stake – her profession, her self-worth. Raw terror, gray fingers of ghost tentacles reaching into her chest, speeding the beating of her heart. She could feel Dr Jake's eyes on her. She willed her eyes to meet his face.

He was leaning forward, eyes fixed on her. "Panic?" he asked softly.

"Feels like that, yeah. I really screwed up, right?" in a child's quaky voice. "I'm in big trouble." She tried to control the quivering of her lips. "I'm - I didn't - could I be sued? Lose my license even?" Waves of panic iced her veins.

Dr. Jake spoke straight, eyes steady. "It all depends on how Lisa rolls this out, how vicious she wants to be. She could make trouble in court. She could subpoena your records of the sessions and get some muckraker lawyer to pick them over to find the flaws. She could summon character witnesses, disgruntled clients she could dig up from the community, or colleagues who've got a beef with you. It may be time to talk to a lawyer just to get your legal options on the table *and* give your fears a little reality check. I'll give you a recommendation." He scribbled a name on the back of an envelope. "Same one who walked me through this process." He looked over his glasses rim steadily, handing her the envelope.

Her head snapped forward. "*You* went through this too?" *Please say yes. God would that comfort my terrified soul that feels so alone in this shit-storm.*

"I did, and only a couple years ago. So when I told you I'd be with you through this, I meant it. Not fun times. I thought I'd wet my pants a few times. Or worse, the truly stinky stuff. So your panic is not crazy and not alone. Our profession has grown a lot more litigious in these greedy times. Lawyers gotta make a living, you know," he smirked.

Jillian shook her head slowly, palms flat on her thighs, closed her eyes and felt her jaws working. And then a chuckle burst through the angst like a bubble of mirth rising. She looked up at Dr. Jake with crinkling eyes. "So people actually live through this – or maybe just one person?"

He squinted at her, took a swig of now-cold coffee and grimaced, then said simply, "Yeah, one," a crooked smile edging along his lips. "And you have to remember, Jillian. She's the antagonist in this. You are just any convenient target for her loss and rage and you get to decide how to receive her volleys. You gotta remember that you did the best work you knew how to do at the time six months ago. Don't go soft on me now – this is just about how blood-thirsty this woman wants to get."

"Thank you, Dr. Jake," she whispered. "That really helps. I was so afraid you'd judge me or even fire me. I've never been – accused of something – so heinous – she's rocking my sense of integrity. I guess I've been lucky, right alongside naive. People generally accept – I mean, I've hardly ever had any enemies. And now it feels like everything's – Jordan's work is so – never mind, you don't want to hear all this whining. Sorry. Just fear talking."

"Don't I know about that. Crazy times. The good thing I hear is you're being honest, asking for help, dealing straight up with it. I like that. She can storm the walls of your integrity but - " Dr. Jake raised his yucky cold coffee, toasting her.

"I'll call the lawyer. Thanks so much for your wise help and especially your transparency. It's the grounding I need."

"Call if you need me. Hang tough, Jilllian."

Chapter 18

Sary speaks, which is rare

Sary called Jillian at work.

Jillian stared at the phone before answering. "Hey Mumser. No, it's fine, I'm on lunch break. I've got a slammer of a day. To what to I owe the honor of this surprise call?"

"I'm sorry to bug you at work – I know how busy – I just needed - " and she choked up. "Sorry. Look, call me when you have a little time, I hate to bother you in the midst – bye now." She barely waited for Jillian's goodbye.

A full day of clients left Jillian drained, not remembering her mom's call until dinner. *I'll call her tomorrow first thing*, she thought. The next day was another full load of clients that started with an early arrival, and a difficult report she took home for night work. Two days later she called her mom.

"I am so sorry, Mom, I don't believe it took me -"

"Never mind. Crisis past. Look, I'm up to my ears at the moment, can I call you back?" in a distant voice.

"Yes of course, Mama. And I'm truly sorry." And she was. But after another full day of people's needs . . .

"I know. Call you later." Sary thought awhile after she hung up. She realized she didn't believe Jillian was sorry or that she even gave it much thought.

Two days later Sary did call back, her voice low and tired, her tone too quiet.

"Mama. You sound tired." Jillian winced, realizing she'd dropped this ball badly and for no real reason. "Mama, I'm genuinely sorry I took so long – my bad – I'm just so busy at work. No excuse, I know. Let's schedule something for this weekend, okay?"

"Well. That took the wind out of my anger. I *was* hurt that you didn't get back to me – felt like you didn't care. Sorry to say – I'm – guess I'm playing the victim but there it is. That's what I feel."

"No, no sorry, I was the thoughtless jerk. Some days I feel bone-weary at the end of a full day of people. Feels like I can't pick up a spoon. I'm not excusing it, Mom, and I feel awful to neglect you of all people. So from now on I'll make a way, I *prom*ise."

"Jillie, it's not – I hated to call and ask you for help when it's what you do for others all day long – it's just – I just want to hear you say – say that you love me. Is that so bad?" Stronger voice now.

Silence. "Mom. You're questioning whether I *love* you? It's possible that I might not *love* you? How can that *poss*ibly be a question – you're the dearest and best mom – you've always been so – God I'm amazed – well duh, could it possibly be because I take your love for us so for granted? How *could* you know? And I don't know what it's like on your end because I don't have a daughter." The silence lengthened while they each absorbed this.

"What *do* you need from me, Mama?" Jillian finally asked softly, still squirming in her skin with recognition of her blindness to Sary's needs. *She's always been so right there. Wow. Who knew? And yet it's so obvious, now, how selfish I've been.*

"Just talk some trash to me once in a while. That would do it. And when I let you know I need you, pick up the phone. That call was hard for me to make. That's pretty much it." Sary felt a weight lift out of her heart. She was declaring what she needed for once from her family and oh how wrong it felt. Her mother never would have made such a declaration, never stood up to her father who was king of the roost and don't you forget it.

Jillian made a note: Flowers to Mom. She said, "Mama. You are such a gift, and asking for what you want is revolutionary for you, I sure know that. So thank you, I'm on it. You are The Best of the Best. And you can kick me in the shins if I get sloppy about this ever again."

"Thank you, Jillie. This was big for me, I had no idea how big until it just burst out. Feels revolutionary indeed, and silly, for a mom of my generation. We're supposed to do all the listening and giving – and now that that's out in the open, it looks pretty dumb, pretty one-sided to never ask for what you want. How can anybody know if I don't get it out of my mouth, or my pen? Oh – aha! Maybe that's why I'm a poet – that's my voice. Whoa -"

"Makes sense. And I won't let this happen again, Mama, now that I know, and you can take that to the bank. Thank you – you just modeled *grit* for me. *Cojones*, Lucia would say," laughing. "Brass ones, I say." She lifted her chin and determined to be better.

"Now I gotta go deal with that publisher on *my* terms. Kick some butt, take some names, is that how you brazen Gen X-ers call it?"

"Yeah, you do that. Permission granted from Gen X-land. I love you a whole lot, my sweet mama, and thank you for this wake up."

They hung up with satisfied little smiles, more awake to their own hearts. Jillian doodled on the note. *Hm-mm. Something new every day when I pay attention in the now. That's not so hard. Damn.*

Sary pulled her shoulders back and called the publisher to navigate the book contract. She gained a bit of ground. She grinned and left Jillian a voicemail at home that said, "We are onto something here. I tried haggling for more in my contract with the publisher and it flew. Wow. Lookout, Boulder, here I go."

Sary mused with a little smile. *What's that old saying? The child becomes father to the man?*

Chapter 19

Lawyer

B
ack in the office next day, Jillian saw Jordan's call show on her
phone. "Yeah babe. Got about one minute. What's shakin'?" *The
sound of my man still brings a smile to my heart. How lucky am I?*
"Lunch date with Coach Trevalyan at CU today. Any pep talk
you wanta beat into me, my shrinky dink-love? Rusty as I am at
interviewing . . ."

"Yeah." She grabbed the squeeze ball on her desk. "Be your cool self.
What's just opened has its own magic and its own timing . . ." *Where
did **that** come from? The old Jillian would have jumped in with a sackful
of advice and actually believed she was entitled to dispense such pearls
of wisdom. Whoa.*

"You never disappoint, girl. Except that one time back in '93. Been
meaning to chat with you about that . . ."

"Stow it, cowboy. Go get the bloody job. You *know* it's yours. And
you know I *adore* you!" Click. *He's on fire. And my part in this? Just
ears, no mouth. No fixing and clearly no control. Damn. This is starting
to feel like minding my own business. This is so simple – so why'd it take
me forty long years?*

She called Josie and left a voicemail. "Josie-my-friend! I just might be a tad capable of learning this new way of listening to my mate, Jos. Simply open mine ears and duct tape my big fat mouth. It's astonishing the free air space up in that listening zone. And lately Jordan's on fire, looking at a basketball coaching job at CU which he'd love to land. And you know how I made that happen? I did *nothing,* just listened as he figured it out. How simple is that? Yeah, not to be confused with easy, right? Hope you're doing great, girlfriend. Call me when you can and tell me everything. I miss you and our juicy talkin'."

She kneaded her flabby calf muscles, then dialed the lawyer and set up a meeting for Thursday.

~ ~ ~

Promptly at three Merin's office manager ushered Jillian into a charming cranberry and coffee high-ceilinged office lined with bookshelves. Merin sat in a flowery wing-back chair, black shirt with striped vest and jeans, offering her hand with an engaging smile. Jillian noted her long thin neck and hands, her salt-and-pepper hair cut short and smart. The glint of steel braces leaning against Merin's chair caught her eye then.

Something about her eyes – inquisitive? And that set mouth – that's a determined look. I can bet she gets some respect in a courtroom. That helps with these butterflies in my belly.

"Thanks, Melissa," to the departing office manager. "So what's going on, nice and slow and easy, Miss Jillian." She took up a pad and pen from the table beside her.

Forthright relaxed voice, Jillian thought. She folded her arms and told Merin the story of the work with Bill and of Lisa's reaction since his death.

Merin raised her eyebrows and made some notes on her pad. "Dr. Tillson is your supervisor and he referred you to me."

"Yes ma'am. One of my notes here is about Bill talking with his wife about investing her money in 'more aggressive' ways. A month later he reported, 'Lost ground with latest investment. Not sleeping well.

Drinking more.' He never came out and called it gambling, but I hear from his neighbor that that was the word on the street. He may have encountered an irrevocable loss that day and freaked out."

Merin rubbed her brow with long fingers. "Fill me in on the threats from his widow."

Jillian brought out copies of emails and a call log and walked them over.

Merin read for several minutes. "Okay. So far we have nothing but hearsay and speculation. That won't hold up in court if that's all Lisa has to go on, Jillian. Sometimes the smoke and bluster are all the threats come to, but I think you're wise to prepare yourself and to know how we'll proceed if it comes to that. We have no action to take yet but do pack that file with *all* correspondence. It'll make my job easier, and cheaper, and you'll sleep better," with a little smile. "I'll need a check for three thousand if you decide to retain me. For now, let's wait and watch to see what she comes up with. Are we on the same page so far?"

She's tough and smart and efficient. She'll do fine, Jillian decided, trying to choke down the fear about the retainer.

"So Lisa doesn't have a case, you're saying. And will malpractice insurance help with your fee?" Jillian knew this was fear asking for reassurance.

"Not so far she doesn't. Let's just see if she comes up with anything substantial or if she's spilling her wind prematurely – that's a sailing metaphor, you understand. Then the retainer and we get to work. And yes, insurance should help, depending on how your policy is written. Any questions at all?"

"I think we're good, Merin. Thanks a lot. This is helpful."

~ ~ ~

She arrived home to a somber Jordan walking Sky around the pasture surrounded by golden sunset light, scattered pink clouds, swallows gathering bugs for a last feed of the night. "Hey cowboy. How'd it go at CU?" She gave him and Sky kisses.

"Well, if you really want to know, it went g-r-r-**reat!**" Sky startled and threw up his head. "Oh, sorry, buddy." He patted Sky's shoulder. "Okay my man?"

"So? Any plans?" *He's holding out. He wants me to pull it out of him.* She took Sky's face in her hands. A fly buzzed around his ears and she swatted at it. "Well hotshot?"

"I took it, Jillie."

She squealed "Oh my Go-od!" She knelt to feel Sky's leg, palpating it.

"I like this guy Trevalyan, Jill. Long time head coach from Baylor, came up here to retire. Long tall Texan with slow speech and a quick mind, seems pretty easy to work with. We hit it off pretty well. The money's good, fifties, part time with possibilities. "I'll coach jv. The guy they hired got a full-time offer from his old school, Wyoming, and had to take it. I start next month."

She stood and wrapped her arms around him. "Thanks be to the God of basketball. You rock, man, I swear. Doesn't he, Sky-buddy? Think I should take him out to dinner? **Cel-e-braaa-tion** Come on!" she sang. Sky threw up his head again. "Your mom and dad are cra-zee, Sky, but you knew that."

~ ~ ~

The restaurant was dim and cozy, not crowded. They favored it for the grilled salmon and excellent service.

Jordan talked all the details out excitedly at dinner, downright loquaciously for him. Jillian feasted on his enthusiasm, staring across the table and recognizing how heavily the worry had been pressing on those shoulders. He took a guzzle of wine, swished it from cheek to cheek and smirked at her. "You think in all this happy horseshit I forgot your lawyer appointment, don'tcha? *Don'*tcha? Talk to me."

"I just love seeing you like this, dude. You light up this dark room for miles."

"Don't change the subject. How was she – a she, right?"

"She was really sharp, tough and crispy clear like we picture lawyers should be. Like Grandpa Clark only nice. Nobody's fool in court if I need her. She moves around with crutches, she's got these long thin hands and she's pretty and forty-fiveish." She took a bite of salad. "Says Lisa doesn't have a case yet, all smoke so far, but she's there if. Retainer of three thou, which I guess is fair market. She'll do just fine. She took the jitters outa my hair. That and the fact that the esteemed Dr. Jake went through this, and she was his counsel, so I trust that recommendation."

"I know you've been lying awake at night – I feel you. I expect this job will take some pressure off you?"

"Oh God yes, already has, just seeing you so happy. And not having to sweat that hefty retainer." She lifted her glass to him. "Here's lookin' atcha, coach."

Chapter 20

Fresh view

Next morning Jillian drove to her office in the stillest of sunlit mornings, musing on the events of yesterday. *Jordan's new job on the top of my grateful-for pile – it registers way deep down in my heart like a pure satisfaction, an unmerited gift. Was that Your work, Whoever You Are? If that's so, then you're making a believer of me. Because that job came out of the blue to save my horse, our farm, and Jordan's happiness. Radford – that beautiful man-spirit – he gets the gold for that connection. We gotta do something really nice for them – send them on a romantic getaway maybe. As soon as we get this lame-ass legal crap behind us.*

And her second thought: *No, now. Can't wait for that, that's just procrastination and indefinite. Rad didn't wait, he jumped in when needed, and he stayed with Jordan all these lean months.*

Her mind stalled there for a time, belly churning up fear and wrestling her peace of mind to the ground. *Ah crap. What defense do I really have – I missed Bill's clue flat out. He was **telling** me he was speculating with Lisa's money, though he did it sideways. And he **told** me he was drinking more and not sleeping – but hold on – Dr. Jake said six months is way too long to hold therapy responsible for a client's progress.*

Is that true? What have I observed all these years in practice? What does common sense tell me?

She drove distractedly into town as her mind wrestled with the two sides of the question. She walked to her office and turned the key. Ahh! She dropped her stuff on her desk and grabbed her cheeks – *Ouee! Well all right then! Epiphany.*

She grabbed a pen and pad to get this down before she forgot.

1 - I am not responsible for Bill Driver's choices six months after I treated him. Whoa. Of course that's true. That's half a year of living and lots of stuff I couldn't know unless he told me. And so much happened since.

2 - I will call Lisa and ask for a lunch meeting on neutral ground out of town. I will not be driven by this damned fear. I will take the high road of compassion.

3 - I will invite her to an honest conversation. Simply that. She can do what she likes with that – scream at me and slam down the phone, continue the madness, whatever. But I am not a victim and I'm not gonna act like one another damn DAY. Whough wough!– done. DAMN. See, Mom? I can learn from your grit.

She slammed the pad down laughing, grabbed her purse and her Jackie Onassis sunglasses and strode down the tree-shaded street for a celebratory Starbucks.

"Miss Jillian? The usual? What, you're traveling incognito? Star status I ain't heard about?" The grinning clerk winked and fixed her mocha latte, brought it over and clamped a lid on it. "You win the lottery?"

"Kind of, Jamie. Just popped my head outa my hindquarters, didja hear it? Sweet day to ya', darlin'," and she sailed out the door.

*So it shows, this clarity, this good energy. That's cool – good energy begets more good energy. How very simple is that? All I have to do is to let that fear work its way through me until I figure out a solution – and it sucks so bad it **demands** the relief of a solution – and then I follow that* *inner guidance.* She reached her office and let herself in, flopped in her chair, and relished the first sip of great coffee.

I just learned a powerful new truth. Where's that bloody phone?

She dialed Lisa and left a voicemail: "Lisa this is Jillian Nicholson. Would you like to have lunch one day in the next couple of weeks? I believe you have my number." She hung up. *Now. Up to her. Shaking a tad inside but I think I got the tone right – willing to move ahead in strength. Friendly but no nonsense. That was me on that phone?*

Mother Teresa said something I heard once – um, oh yeah. 'We are not called to be successful, just faithful.' Lisa can do with this as she likes. I'm doing this because it's the next right thing for me. Yeah – the monkey's gone from my back – oh yeah, oh yeah. She danced around triumphantly. *In Your court now, You Whoever. And, um, thank you. You seem to be working some magic in me, some sense of beyond-fear. A tiny strand of trust, maybe? Healing a layer of fear that I've run from since Baby Judd died and my little-girl world fell apart?*

Chapter 21

Jeb

A few days later Jillian was waiting for her next appointment when the phone rang. Caller ID announced it as Jeb, her dad. "Hey Daddy! How's my favorite horse thief?" *This is rare. Something must be up.* She gazed at the pastel above her desk whose bucolic tones always offered peace, serenity. *Muted blues and greens give me hope somehow.*

"Sounds great. How about the hearty lunches at the Boulderado for you steak and potato lovers? Good salads too. See you there at one? Thanks for calling, dear old dad." She hung up and tipped her chair back, fingers massaging her neck as she stared at the ceiling. *Is this a first ever, or at least a lo-ong time. Listen up time, for sure.*

The door opened and her next client hour began. She hustled up the street to lunch afterward.

"Hiya Daddy-o. How are you, honey?" She reached for the hug that lingered between them before they sat down. "I was trying to remember – how long has it been since we had a date, just the two of us?"

"Last century," he said gravely. There were horses involved as I recall." He smiled his old warm smile and picked up his menu. "That's my fault, Sugar. Not that I didn't want to but – you know how it goes..."

He's aged – more gray – and he looks what, sad? No. Old? That's new. Still that same wise thoughtful look, those straight-into-you brown eyes, but the lines between his eyes have deepened, now that I really look. He's gotta be, what, sixty two, sixty three? Yeah, sixty three. I wonder what this is about. Patience, girl, for this dearly distinguished man who has always been your own dad, your champion.

He was dressed casually in denim shirt and jeans, his mustache bushier, a few more pounds. Nothing outstanding. He still took his time working things through his mind. He gave their orders, gallant as always to the Latino waiter, hazarding a friendly stab at Spanish, then turned his brown eyes full bore on her own.

"Guess you're wondering why I invited you all here," he gestured comically around with a sweep of his hand. She noticed then that his hand was trembling. He saw her notice and put both long hands in his lap.

"What is it, Daddy?" she asked softly.

"Parkinson's, early stages, not bad. Yet. But – I wanted to tell you girls myself, one of you at a time. I'm retiring in three months." He waited for that to sink in.

"Whoa. I won't tell Cal of course, I'll leave that to you. Ah, Dad. That's big. How do you feel about it?"

"God, you're a thoughtful one. When'd you get so mature? Or are we on the clock?" He chuckled, reaching over to take her hand. His hand shook as he held hers. He gently pulled it back.

"Guess I won't be trying that again. I'll spill something nasty on your pretty dress," and they had a real laugh.

"Your idea, this retirement?" She sipped her iced tea. She thought she spotted a jerking wince before he covered it.

He chewed a moment. "Actually no, damn your perceptive questions. Dan, the new young Turk at the helm, is giving several of us long-timers a severance package we can't refuse." He scowled in his best Don Corleone Godfather snarl and twisted his mustache. Jillian cracked up. "So no. I'm being put out to pasture – keep Sky company." He cleared his throat.

"So I'm gonna pester your mom more, fly fish when I want, read all those books piled up by my chair, take up golf or calf-roping or whatever old farts are sent out to do these days." He took up his fork and jabbed at his chicken. "Be-Jaysus it sucks, tell you the truth. Gotta reinvent myself at my ripe old age. But enough whining. Until dessert. Guess I just want you girls' company on this ride. Maybe we'll actually have some time to play now. I miss the hell outa you."

"Dad, you've had one banner year, ain't you. First your dad, then Grandma's cancer, now this. Be-Jaysus indeed!" They howled at the old family cuss that used to drive Sary's father through the roof. "Shanty Irish," he would growl and storm out of the room.

"How's Grandma doing? I saw her last week or two and she brushed it off. She looked maybe a bit lighter but sadder too since Grandpa's gone." She searched his face.

"Yeah," he admitted, forking a fry. "The old rascal sure was high maintenance. I don't know how she kept her sanity all these years. You think she was for real or faking it for appearances sake? She's not real, uh, pushy, more of a giver, right?"

"Oh, she was real all right. Just not around him. She was herself and fun with us. Admitted how ornery he was and plotted all kinds of mean comebacks, but then she always laughed. She loved him in spite of himself, is what we got from her."

"Yeah, I realized you kids saw a different side of her than anybody else got, not that she wasn't a great mom. But you girls are the cat's meow to her. Your mom woulda pushed him off the nearest cliff many a day. 'Why did those poor little girls have to strike out with both grandpas?' she'd bitch to me every time one of them showed his face. Which wasn't often, thankfully." They laughed easily about family foibles.

"Ah, Dad. You and Mama are such great parents, especially against the backdrop of such tough old geezer dads. Thanks, my hero, ya' done real good." She grabbed his hand and held on as it shook. He let her. She brushed quickly at her cheek with her sleeve, then brought his shaking hand to her lips.

"Now don't start gushin'. You know I can't handle a gushin' broad.

Never could. Have to get you a bunch of those blue irises or somethin' you love to shut you up." He looked around to see who might be watching, wiped his trembling hand over his face, took a swig of beer, and grinned at his daughter.

"There. I'm glad that's done. Thanks, honey. Hope Callie takes it as well as you did. So – how's that business about the client suicide coming along?" He lowered his voice to barely audible.

"It's been quiet lately. I found a good lawyer, Merin Dunfrey? You know her?"

"No, I don't know the criminal folks anymore. Nobody not already in mothballs." He raised an eyebrow.

"Well, she's sharp and I think she'll be tough in court if it comes to that." She took a bite of salad. "I invited the adversary-lady, the widow of the suicide? To lunch." She twinkled to him.

"That's my girl. De-escalate. Brilliant. And cheap." He raised his beer to her. "To mediation."

"Yeah, it feels right. This whole twisted mess is keeping me awake, so I figure it's gotta be far worse for her. I think she just wants somebody to hang – whoa, that's not funny – to pay for his death and her loss. She really loved – no, she loves him still. Merin Dunfrey I think it was, or maybe my supervisor, Dr. Jake, said this is how rich people deal with pain. Slap it in court."

"Yeah, there's a lot of that in courts. Your grandpa *told* some stories about rich folks in court. I think that's what soured me on corporate law. It sounded like a gold-plated Monopoly game to my young do-gooder ears. Us young upstart law lackeys were about world-changing, by damn. You gotta remember, this was the sixties when nobody over thirty knew anything to us radical scouts. We knew it *all*. Man we had some dinner table go-rounds. Mom hadda pull us off each other many a night." He drew on his beer.

"Maybe that's how we held together, Dad and me. We were passionate about what law could do for the world from our opposite corners and we were dead-sure we were right, but then we had to consider each other's ideas though we hated them. Come to think of it, he sharpened my arguments by challenging every damn thing I said. Hmm – never thought of it quite like that. You make me think, girl. How'd you do that?"

"You're clever, dear old dad. Oh, sorry, that wasn't funny either." She covered her grinning mouth and they laughed out loud. "I love you, Daddy. You're one cool fun buzzard."

"Yeah, well don't let that get out. Dessert? So I c'n whine some more?"

Chapter 22

Lunch

Two weeks later. Jillian was eating a chicken soup lunch in her office when it suddenly came to her. *I haven't heard a thing from Lisa in two weeks. No threats, no emails. Wonder what that signals. I can only hope it says she's thinking about my lunch offer, reworking her position. Or she's reloading. God.*

As if on cue her phone rang, startling her out of the meditation. She answered it and heard a low familiar rasp coming slowly through. "Jillian?"

Lisa! she registered. *As if I summoned her by thinking . . . I guess I did.*

"This is Lisa . . . Lisa Driver."

Jillian took a shaky breath, reaching for her squeeze ball, her heart cranking up to staccato range. *Easy, girl. Hear her out.* "Hi, Lisa. Thanks for calling back."

"I could do lunch next Wednesday at one at the Hideaway in Broomfield if that works for you. On Table Mesa, you know it?" Her voice was low and slow, that familiar gravelly tone, nervous.

Jillian reached for her planner. "Yes I know the place. Just give me a minute – yes, that's good, but I'll need travel time – can we make it one fifteen? I'll have nearly two hours then so we're not rushed."

"Yes, one fifteen is fine. See you then." Click.

Jillian sucked in her lips and raised her eyebrows. *God I'm as nervous as she sounds. Her fear was tangible – I gotta give her major credit for guts to call. So now to my business. What **am** I so shaky about? Meeting my demon fear, a little phone call like that. Nah, it's bigger. Maybe it's that I'm learning a whole new way, a way of courage. Responding rather than reacting. Big girl pants.*

This deserves focused attention. How about I try meditating on it? She closed her eyes and dropped down inside, letting deep slow breaths come on their own time and simply following them.

After several minutes she was aware of Bill's presence, close, palpable. She peeked to see if he was in the flesh right across from her like in their sessions. Nothing. *Whoa – but that's truly his spirit. I just smelled his flippin' Old Spice! And there I feel his special energy, his intense gray eyes looking out the window as he often did. His favorite green Tartan flannel sleeves rolled up his forearms. Small wonder Lisa is so baffled by this embezzlement stuff. Bet she thinks he's above the screw ups of an ordinary human.*

Eyes closed, she could hear him say, "I don't know how to recoup this – my cousin drained the well dry, the sorry son-of-a-bitch. Oh, beg pardon, Miss Jillian. And right under my nose for God's sake – what an idiot!" He smacked his head with the heel of his palm.

"He is. I'm just sayin'. A sorry s.o.b." She raised an eyebrow. "Despicable. I love saying that word. Des**pic**able. So what does Lisa know about the shortfall, Bill?" *Amazing how intricate this conversation, and how it feels just like an actual talk we had. Was it the same conversation I'm remembering or a new one?*

"She never wanted me to bring him into the business, never trusted him, so she gets that I-told-you-so look and doesn't wanta hear it. She knows I'm under water but doesn't want to know details. You know, I sense she kind of love/hates her money, so she leaves it to me to handle, but I better not screw up. So I scramble alone as if I'm the idiot who created this whole goddam stupid shebang."

"You resent that, having no support from her?" *I believe I said those very words. This is truly weird . . .*

Bill looked at her long, pondering that. He had come to realize the depth of inquiry in her questions and to give them their due. He took a long moment to sit with that.

She watched his body signals as she waited. *Is that a new tic at the corner of his mouth?*

"Good one, Jillian. Yeah, I do. It never occurred to me that I deserved her support in this, but I do, right? It's just one more human foible – God forbid I should show her any weakness." He scratched an itch on his cheek. "I'd support her if she were in a freakin' jungle like this. Come to think of it, this really *sucks*. I'm *not* the loser of the western world and I don't deserve that. If anything, I'm the *victim* of the slimy weasel, and I'm learning stuff like everybody else in this dizzy damn planet we call Life."

"Right on, Bill. Sounds like a conversation for you and Lisa to begin, you think?"

She felt him fade away and knew the vignette was complete. *Wow. What was that? I never experienced anything like that before. I **like** it – it's connecting to something far beyond me. I need to kick this around with somebody, but who?*

~ ~ ~

She found Lisa at the Hideaway in a booth in back. "Sorry, Lisa. Traffic was bad." *Calm yourself, girl. She can't beat you. Not in a public venue anyway and not in Boulder.*

"No problem, Jillian. I just got here too, same problem." She folded her hands in front of her mouth, looking away. "How have you been?" Dark eyes under white baseball cap darting in and away.

She looks apprehensive and exhausted. This has to be so tough for her, to be grieving, raw, to have lost so much and now to show up for this difficult conversation. "Thanks a lot for coming, Lisa. I truly respect that." She looked straight in Lisa's eyes. She shook out her napkin and laid it in her lap.

"I'm pretty well, all things considered, thanks for asking. Lost my Grandpa recently, and some changes happening at the ranch, but we're hanging in there so far. And you?" *Play it light. Don't dive into the deep water unless she leads you in. Let her pace this – she showed up and that's the first step.*

Lisa offered, voice low, "I'm sorry about your grandpa. There's never a good time to lose a . . ." She looked away, her eyes clouded. It took several minutes to compose herself. "Good I picked this dark place for privacy." Her mouth twitched in a weak smile. "Maybe – hm-mph – you would explain why you asked me to lunch." She bit her lip.

The waitress came for their orders. They both chose the soup and salad bar, made their way through the line and returned to their booth in silent thought.

Jillian began. "Okay. It's like this, Lisa. I thought a lot of Bill, and I felt I owed it to his memory to honor him in peace if we could. So I come in peace. That's about it." She spooned up some cream of broccoli soup and tasted it. "Mm – good."

Lisa took her time to think, eating her salad, hat brim blocking Jillian's view of her face. Finally she spoke, low and careful. "I wanted to climb into the grave alongside him. He was everything to me – best friend, lover, strength, the only shot at happiness I'd ever even dared to imagine. Life without him? *Shit.* My growing up was – not fun. Parents too hooked on their money and position to pay any attention to us kids, me and my sister. Whoever the hired help was at the time looked after us. I was *so* pissed off my whole life. My sister's turned into a strung-out bipolar druggie. I didn't have a clue what love was, what this hole in my gut was, until Bill came along." She chewed and thought a while.

"So when he – when – *shit* will these tears never end?" She wrestled for calm and then began again. "So I thought my life was over and there hadda be somebody responsible for all this pain, somebody to blame – so you fit the bill because he respected you, said you were the best shrink he'd ever – so there it is. So when you called me, it was the what, intervention I needed. *Stop. Take a look. Is your vengeance strategy working? Are you happier?* It put my choices straight – to keep this damned expensive legal charade rolling or put it on hold and get to the healing I thirst for?" The floodgate released.

This is her amend. She's surrendering. Jesus this is powerful. She reached over to brush Lisa's hand with her fingertips. "That's amazing, Lisa." Hot tears pooled and dropped on Jillian's cheeks. "That's – true chutzpah. Thank you, for real. I don't know if I could be half the woman in your shoes."

"Yeah well – guess I better get to work on this stinkin' grief. Know any good shrinks who could help me shake this shit loose?" She chuckled and attacked her soup, suddenly famished.

Jillian let out her relief in a long rolling laugh. "Yeah, actually I do. I'll give you her contact info before I go. She's excellent. Man – who'd'a thunk we'd be laughing about all this. Thanks, Lisa, this is the damn break I needed."

"No, thank YOU, Jillian. Your simple lunch invite spared us both a whole lotta crap. I was spinning out of control and who knows where that legal bullshit would have taken us? Nowhere good for sure, and nowhere cheap. I had revenge on my mind and it had a fat hook in my lip." She smacked her cheek and held it. "This is good stuff. I've got the tab. You just saved me a boodle."

They ate in silence for a few beats.

Lisa smiled and offered, "The irony of this whole nightmare is, I just learned that if he hadn't offed himself and put the spotlight on him as the screwup, with me in the clear based on my ignorance of what he was doing, I would have lost it all. So that ace of a man took the fall to spare me once again. Now that, Jillian, is love. Strange to have finally found what I was seeking this way."

106

Chapter 23

Sky

Out on the deck early Saturday morning, Jillian was holding a hot strong coffee, journal at hand, sunlight warm on her face. Her eye caught a movement in the pasture, then the sound of ground-pounding hoofbeats. Sky running, head high. He jabbed at the air with hind hoofs.

What the hell? He hasn't run like that in – what's up with that wild dude? She ran out through the barn to the pasture, grabbed a scoopful of mash, and climbed on the fence to watch. *Did I just see what I saw?*

Sky ran up to her and stopped six feet in front with mane and tail flying, head high, triumphant.

She slipped down and walked toward him, holding the mash to her belly, over to where he stood pawing the ground. He never looked more magnificent to her than in that moment.

Tears flowed as she held out the mash to him. "Holy shit, son." She held the mash until he gulped it down, then wiped her hands on her jammies and knelt to palpate the leg. *Here's the break. A little swollen, not like before.* She compared it to the other leg. *Yup, a little swelling.* She watched him as she pressured gently with her fingers. He didn't flinch. "Of course you know your body too well to run like that if you weren't ready, Buddy. Let's get Doc out here, and Jordan, and see what they think. If this is what I think you're trying to tell me, pal, we're goin' up into those hills real soon. *God* you're some incredible horse."

She went in to hustle coffee up to Jordan. "Coach. Hot tip from the pasture. Sky was tearin' it up when I got up, *flyin'* around that pasture. Come see." He laughed that she was all but hopping up and down.

They raced out to Sky. He trotted over, throwing his head up and down as if confirming "Yeup!" to the wonder of this.

Jordan raised his eyebrows. "Sure looks like a healed, ready-to-rock horse to me. Lemme have a look at that leg, bud." He knelt to feel the foreleg with both hands, fingers patient. After several passes, he stood and sniffed the fresh morning. "M'am, I do believe your horse is itchin' to ride. Let's get Doc's say-so just to be sure."

He rubbed Sky's withers and belly, his face lit up from inside. "You are *somethin'* else, you big hunka horseflesh. I figured you'd make it through this. Thank you, son."

Jillian slid under his free arm and put him in an irrepressible squeeze. "This is gonna be one sweet day, babe."

~ ~ ~

Doc stopped in later to prod and poke at the leg. "You big show-off, Skywalker. You are one special breed. I say go do your thing out there and let 'er rip." He stood and brushed his hands on a shop rag. "Let him pace this – I know I'm not tellin' you anything new. He'll ease his own way into *his* new full throttle. He is one cagey city slicker, sure of what he wants. And the leg is far stronger for this setback and healing."

Jillian eased onto his bare back later, the better to sense his body responses. She neck-reined him around the pasture slowly. "I don't believe how sweet this feels, how grateful I am, Big Guy. I thought we had to give up the wonder of... That'll teach *me* to trust. You're stronger than I dared to believe, and all we did was keep you clean and watch you heal," she whispered softy to him.

He nickered and nodded an 'I-know-girlfriend', nodding his big head.

If only I could know his thoughts. He seems to know so much more than a horse is supposed to know, but that's just human speak.

Callie came out after dinner with Marko to show off his new truck, symbol of the new start. Marko bragged, "I'm going American with a Chevy. What do you theenk, Jordan?"

"You're still a frickin' spagetti-munchin' wop, dressed up in shiny black metal or no." He kicked the tire. "There. First ding."

Jillian took her sister out to see Sky. "Lookit that boy, Cal. Frickin' wonder horse. We rode some today and look at him. And you know, as I laid back on his withers and looked at the clouds like we always did? I had this amazing feeling of all being well, and that this was just a taste of it."

"Think he could teach my kids?" Callie quipped.

Chapter 24

Mandy

"**M**andy has what, buddy? You broke up there. Run that by me again." Jordan dragged on his cigarette. This was sounding not good. "Oh man, Radford – oh SHIT," he yelled to the mountains. "Not Mandy. Man, Rad. Not beautiful sweetheart Mandy. Jesus this bites." He was surprised when his eyes filled. Of all the best people in the world – who doles these for-shit cards out? And why, goddammit?

He listened as Rad's deep tone came again. "They think they got it early enough that it ain't spread, that this is all of it. We'll see. I, uh, wanted to see if you were in a position to help at all – sure hate askin' but . . ."

"Of course, man. Thanks to you I can. How much do you need?"

"Could you loan me a couple grand for these medical bills? I know it's been tight . . ."

"I'll send you the job-finder's fee we've been thinkin' about. We were talkin' about what to do since you saved my butt with this coaching gig. So I'll do the best I can – and it's a gift. I owe you the pick of the litter at least. And Rad, I'll – hm-mm – I'll be prayin' for you guys. I – I love you man."

"Thanks, Jordo. I'm kinda thin in the folks I can ask department. 'Preciate it."

Two days later Radford found an envelope written in Jordan's jerky scrawl in the mail. He took it to the hospital to open with Mandy. *I got a good feelin' about this,* he thought, and stuck it in his pocket.

"How're you doin' today, Sugar?" He bent to kiss her, then stood tall and held her cheek in his big palm.

'I'm better every day. I know cuz' I'm cranky as hell in this loony bin. Some of these nurses – iyee!" She shook her hand out, laughing with her eyes. " Doc said one more day and I'm out of here, you believe that? What's new out there in the unreal world? What's that stickin' out of your pocket?" She adjusted her gown, flirting unsubtly. "Sure am glad to know I get to love on *you* a while longer."

He fished the envelope out of his pocket and offered it to her. She shook her head. "What's this? You look. Can't read that man's writing no way."

He slit open the side and slid the check out. "Whoa." His head jerked up. "Looka here. Five thousand. And it says gift." He slid down into the chair, hands on his knees, staring at the check that felt like platinum. "That there's back wages and then some," he said.

"That's right and it's fair, Rad. You saved his ass and not for the first time. You were stretchin' yourself, helpin' out a white man, a boss yet. This's paybacks. All those months he couldn't pay what he owed you, don't forget those peanut butter dinners."

"I did what anybody would have, and I passed on information that was meant for him. A conduit is all. He'd do the same. He just did."

"Yeah. You trust him 'cause he's earned it. And you did it with your own – uhm, generosity. Yeah, that's the word. Don't it feel good? Sure looks good *on* you." She was grinning that ever-ready grin that he never tired of.

He raised an eyebrow, then softened into a half smile. "This'll get us started on these bills and the insurance will knock off a chunk. Man this takes a load off. Oh, and he told me to tell you Skywalker's leg healed up strong so Jillian's ridin' 'im." He looked out the window, licking his teeth. "How the hell'd I git a white man for a friend?"

"Man, that's so good. That powerful damn horse – well shit, Rad, that big horse ain't gonna best me. You watch me. I need me some actual medicine to start my soul healin' – sun and trees and blue sky and herbs and good lovin'. I *know* what to do. I'm done with this sick shit and hospitals. You hear me, baby? We're gonna *beat* this starting *today*."

He sat basking in her, wondering why she was given to him, he who'd had few bright moments to remember. And now she was given back from death.

I don't think I earned her, that ain't how it works. Just loved my way in somehow. No figurin' it.

~ ~ ~

Jillian worked over every inch of Sky's hide with meticulous care this August morning. Every neglected detail – teeth, eyes, hooves, penis shaft, tail – got the soapy rag or brush, wiping away the dust and detritus from months of pasture rolling and rest. He let her, even seemed to enjoy it, standing still for his touch flesh quivering.

She chattered to him. "This is a new beginning for me and you, big. We're gonna ease up into those hills we love today, you and me. What's it been, six, seven months you've been gettin' a free lunch? And I doubted every day - okay, I know, dopey doubter me – that this day would come. Forgive me? Your unshakable ability to heal yourself – you are my power totem, my guru, the dearest four-legged friend of my life, buddypal. And now you're Mandy's hero too – but no pressure." She peered into his eyes and saw irony.

Time to bridle and mount up. He didn't wince as she hoisted herself onto his bare back. "Oh God, Sky, this feels so right. Let's go see how the trail's looking." She guided him slowly up the trail, more filled in now with high grass and branches. "Easy, Kimosabe," she crooned to him. "Let's underplay this ride if anything. If we ever louse this up again . . ."

She feasted on the view, on the feel of his ribs and his long-gaited walk, the birdsongs, the clear air gentle on her face. *I am the most blessed of women. I live here in this lovely land with you, you wonderhorse. And Jordie. God this is good.*

They reached the summit outcropping of granite and stood surveying the vista. She lay back on his haunches and basked in the sun on her face and arms and legs, his warm back, her hands dangling to contact his flesh.

So. Surveying my small world, my queendom, I am at peace. Unmerited and unhoped for even, dummy that I was.

"If it never gets any better than this, Sky buddy, I'm grateful for this day."